Their Wicked Wolf

Mystic Wolves 6
Elle Boon

Dedication

Every story I write seems to come from another story in the series. Well, Sky has been that story just waiting to be written. I put it on the back burner, thinking this and that needed to be written first, but finally she started to scream at me, or should I say River and Raydon did. Now I am so excited I listened to my muse, or should I say muses. One of the things I think I say a lot is "When life throws you a curve, you swerve with it." Let me tell you, I'm a professional swerver by now. I know most people say when life gives you lemons, make lemonade. Nope, I say pass me the vodka and let's get this party started. I hope y'all enjoy Sky and her guys as much as I enjoyed digging deep into their stories. Get ready for a truly wicked story and grab onto whatever is near because there's bound to be some swerving and possibly the need for alcohol.

Love y'all so hard
Elle

Other Books by Elle Boon

Wild and Dirty

SEAL Team Phantom Series

Delta Salvation

Delta Recon

Delta Rogue

Delta Redemption

Mission Saving Shayna

Protecting Teagan

The Dark Legacy Series

Dark Embrace

Prologue

Every bone in her body was breaking, sweat pouring off her as she lay immobile, thinking if she didn't move it wouldn't hurt quite so badly, but she knew better. She knew the pain wouldn't ease until her best friend healed. *Goddess, why would a father do this to his child?*

Sky moaned out loud, then sucked her lips between her teeth, holding the sounds inside as best she could. If her parents heard, they'd freak the fuck out. Not because they cared, but because they would hate for her to interrupt their lives anymore than she already did, and that was the last thing she needed. If she wanted to continue being friends with Taryn, she'd have to suffer in silence like their alpha said, *"You want to be friends with my mutt, then you'll pay the price. You willing to pay, little bitch?"* Keith asked coolly. Was she willing to accept the pain mentally and internally, while he inflicted even worse on his daughter physically? The answer was yes, had been yes since he'd first asked. Sometimes, like now when the ability to breathe was almost too great, she regretted her bargain with the devil named Keith, but then she'd watch in horror the nightmare Taryn lived with, and she'd given a silent nod, knowing the bastard was aware, knowing he would be waiting to share the punishment he doled out to his daughter with Sky as well.

Hours later she lay panting, her heart beating too fast, but the need to get up and go see her friend and tend to her very real wounds, had her swinging her legs over the side of the bed. A wave of dizziness made Sky suck in a deep breath before she could get up. "Good Goddess, what did he do this time?" she questioned the empty room. Using her arms to shove herself up, pain shot from her fingers to her shoulders, the screams she'd held inside escaped.

"Sky, are you alright?" Her mother's shrill voice asked through the door.

She bit her bottom lip, stilling the tremble. "Yeah, I must've fallen asleep and got up too quickly. My foot's gone numb, and you know how

7

I seem to fall all the time." As far as excuses went it was lame, but her mother would buy it.

"Well, be more careful. I was cooking and almost burned myself."

The sharp retort made fresh tears track down her face. Where once her mother used to hug and coddle her, now she was remote, almost loveless toward Sky. She hated Keith with every fiber of her being. He was not only an awful father, and cruel leader, but he was evil to his core. Why couldn't the adults, the ones who were supposed to protect the innocents, see that? Instead, they let him hurt those weaker than him, taking pleasure in others pain and suffering in front of the entire pack, and what he did behind their backs had to be worse. The bargain he made with Sky...she shuddered and closed off what she'd agreed to do in order to continue her friendship with Taryn, his daughter. If her taking on even a little of what the other girl felt eased some of her suffering, she'd do it, which was what she did. Silently. How Taryn could stand the actual physical pain was beyond Sky's imagination.

She took her first tentative step, feeling aches in every joint, throbbing in every cell of her body seemed to shout with each move she made. "For fuckssake, what the hell is Taryn going through?"

Once in the bathroom, she inspected herself in the mirror. Like every other time, she didn't look as though she'd been beaten, not like Taryn, not on the outside. Inside however, was a different story. Where nobody could see, she knew she had more than a few bruised ribs and possibly even more internal damage.

With Keith, one never knew exactly what you'd get. However, he wouldn't want to alert the pack to what he'd done. Of course, he was alpha, so he could do anything he wanted. The thought sickened her, knowing he could and would do what he pleased, and nobody would stop him, not even her parents. She splashed water on her face, pulled her hair into a ponytail, then left without looking too closely at her image. Keith had a mate once, Taryn's mother, but he didn't care who he forced a mating with for the night, only drawing a line with age. She shuddered at the thought of what it meant to be with the vile beast. "I'll kill myself first," she vowed, uncaring if he caught the thought.

By the time she made it to where Taryn lay, her bones had cracked like she'd been to a chiropractor, making her sigh in relief. Damn, how many more times could she go through...she stopped the thought before it could finish. For Taryn, she'd go through the same thing she'd gone through over and over again, like she'd done for the past ten years or so. She just hoped her body held out. An anguished cry escaped her at the sight of Taryn lying motionless in the center of the gathering. All around pack members stood, staring at the alpha's daughter, yet none moved to help her.

Movement from the other side showed Joni entering. Neither of them said a word as they gathered the battered and broken form of Taryn up from the ground, ignoring the blood pouring from wounds too numerous to count. The crowd of gawkers parted for them, eyes evading them as if they were ashamed. Sky wanted to shout that yes they should be, but her own body still ached.

"She's still alive, Sky, so stop with the heavy breathing like you're about to breakdown," Joni ordered.

If only Joni knew the heavy breathing was due to the bruised ribs and the injured lungs still trying to heal themselves. She felt his evil eyes staring at her, knew he was commanding her to look toward him. Sky's head inched to the right, her eyes finding the malevolent gaze of Keith the bastard. His stare held her spellbound for precious seconds while a fist seemed to wrap around her throat, making it hard for her to breathe. *"Remember our bargain, little bitch, or the life you hold will be no more."* His deep gravelly voice in her head made her hold Taryn too tightly, causing her best friend to flinch even though she didn't wake. Sky didn't know if Keith meant her life, or his daughter. Either one, she didn't want to lose. Not yet.

Several days later, after she and Joni worked to keep Taryn as comfortable as possible, their friend woke a changed woman. Sky could tell their life would be forever altered as she looked into the beautiful eyes of one of the only true friends she had. Even though they'd not been allowed to do much together, Taryn had been the one person she'd held closest to her heart, besides Joni. The only other person she'd give her life for. A stab of fear wormed its way through her. Sky had a feeling it would be her life that would be forfeit if Taryn found a way to escape, for Keith would look for a new chew toy. He wouldn't look too far since he knew Sky could handle his punishments without complaint, at least the ones on the inside. Goddess, she didn't want to contemplate going through what Taryn did, but she also wanted her friend free, even if it meant her life. Heck, she didn't have much of one anyhow.

"Thank you, jeezus. I didn't think you'd ever wake the fuck up. I swear you scared like ten years off my life," Joni said, coming to stand beside Taryn, a glass in her hand.

"How long was I out?"

"Three motherfucking days," Sky growled. The longest three days of her life with Keith beating at her head asking for updates. Finally, she'd opened up, allowing him to feel everything she did. The recoil of shock and...horror was almost worth the backlash she'd received.

Taryn tried to sit up at the announcement. "What? I didn't wake at all?"

"I almost hauled your ass in to the hospital. One more day and you were going." Joni held the drink out, the anxiety she'd obviously felt clear in her tone. "Drink this, and then you need to eat, and no you didn't wake."

Taryn gulped the juice down, her eyes blinking back tears.

"How do you feel?" Sky asked, although she already knew the answer.

Taryn stretched her legs out, followed by her arms, smiling broadly. "Damn, I feel pretty good for a chick who just got run over by a truck."

The feel of Keith's hands wrapping around her throat kept her from responding for a few seconds. Finally, she licked her lips and tried again. "We took turns watching you, making sure none of the assholes decided to come in and take advantage of you. The second day, we decided to wash you up a bit. I couldn't stand to look at the blood on you a moment longer, but we didn't want to jar you too much. Do you think you're up for a bath?" Sky asked. Someday she'd make a great mate, just not to one of the jackholes in their pack. Of course, if Keith had his way, she'd be one of his stable of women. Bile rose up at the thought.

"I'd love a bath, but I don't have one. A quick shower will suffice though. You two best be getting back to your places. I don't want you getting into trouble on my behalf."

Sky could've told her she was already paying a price for her friendship, but she'd never do that to her. For one, Keith would know, and goddess only knew what he'd do to them both. For another, Taryn already suffered too much. "Taryn, you're always welcome in my home, you know that." Her parents would fall all over themselves if they thought Keith would pay them favors for allowing his daughter in their home.

Like always, her friend waved aside the offer, making excuses and shooing them out the door. Another piece of her heart broke at the loss of her friendship. For her, Taryn and Joni were the only light in her world.

"We'll see you in a day or so. Rest and eat, woman." Joni shook her finger at Taryn, hurrying out of the small space ahead of Sky.

"When will I see you again?" The question slipped out before she could stop it. Knowledge was power. On one hand she wanted the answer, but on the other she didn't. Keith could and would pull it from her if she knew.

"I'll be in touch. I just need...I need a little time." Taryn raised her hand, smoothing her palm over Sky's head. "Take care of you, Sky."

"You're leaving." Sky stated.

Taryn didn't deny her words.

Before she could make a fool of herself, she wrapped her arms around Taryn's stomach and gave her a quick hug. "Take care of you." Sky turned and hurried out the door, feeling Taryn stare as she nearly ran all the way home. Goddess, she was such a pussyass little bitch. She should've told Taryn. She should've explained about the bargain she'd made with Keith all those years ago. Now, it was too late, and she had a sinking feeling that when Taryn disappeared, Keith would come looking for a new body to replace his favorite punching bag, for when he needed to beat his anger out. Only Sky wasn't as strong as Taryn.

Chapter One

Sky smiled at Talia, her friend Taryn's mother, her savior. It had been months since Keith's death. Goddess, she finally felt as if her world was going to be bright again after so much darkness. "How're you liking Mystic Lodge so far?" she asked the older woman.

It had taken Sky a couple months to acclimate herself to the new normal, but now she felt as if she was...steady. No longer did she flinch at a raised voice or the slamming of doors.

Talia smiled. "I'm still trying to take it all in. There's so much to see and learn. Of course, it'll be worth it once my girls...anyway, it's beautiful up here."

She totally understood what Talia had said, and what she hadn't. Taryn and her other daughter Taya were both mated to Mystic Pack members, but it had taken them a little to warm up to their mother.

"Are you two just standing around gabbing? Don't you have work to do?" The anger coming from the manager was new and off-putting, something Sky wasn't sure she could deal with much longer. Yes, she liked working at the lodge, but she wouldn't stay if she had to work for the man much longer. He'd been fine until a month or so ago.

"We're on our appointed break, which is our legal right to do," she said, glad her voice didn't crack.

Talia put her hand up, stopping him from whatever he'd been about to say. "Can you tell me again the number of guests we're expecting?"

Sky didn't stick around to hear whatever else was said. Her job didn't include office duties, not like Talia's. No, she was in charge of nothing too important, other than making sure the front of the lodge was kept up to standards. Meaning she was a glorified cleaning lady. She didn't mind though since she could blend into the woodwork when she wanted. Unlike Talia who'd been held as a prisoner for over twenty-five years, beaten, broken, and worse, by Keith her supposed mate, yet she was willing to step in when Sky cowed away. "Goddess, I'm sick of being such a little bitch like he called me."

She went outside, hoping the fresh air would clear her head. She'd go for a drive in her Beamer, her one luxury she still had thanks to her parents being smart enough not to give Keith all their money. Goddess, just thinking the bastards name made her stomach roll.

Her mind went back to the last time she'd driven the winding roads. Only then she'd been running from something. No, she'd been running from someone, make that two someones. Hell, she didn't know what was up and what was down, only remembered the need to flee and she had, nearly killing herself in the process by running head first into a diesel. Luckily for her, the driver had been more aware of the road. She'd been able to swerve back into her own lane in time, barely missing a head-on collision. Sometimes, Sky wondered if everyone wouldn't be better off if she weren't around.

She'd even thought she could run off to Texas, losing herself among the millions of people there. It had been a pipe dream as Keith had been waiting for her when she'd returned, his need to feel flesh under his fists and claws were great that evening. "Don't think about it or him. He's gone and can't hurt you or anyone anymore." She shuddered.

"Who're you talking to, little lamb?"

Sky spun around, coming face-to-face with a man she'd never met. Power pulsed off him, making what Keith had seem miniscule in comparison. "Pardon me, I didn't see you there."

The man floated forward. "Of course you didn't, because I didn't want you to. What's your name, little lamb?"

Breath froze in her throat the closer he got. His nickname for her made her feel as if it was prophetic. A lamb being led to slaughter flashed before her eyes.

"I see you understand me very well," he murmured, standing in front of her.

"I have to go back to work." She spun on her heel, running as fast as she could back to the lodge, back toward the safety of where she'd last seen Talia.

The door to Dave's office was open, the scent of the manager and fear filling the air. She didn't understand why they'd hired a human to run the place, but he seemed nice enough. However, he'd become a first class porchdick lately, but stepping into his office, the sight of him lying on the floor had her almost panic shifting. The next thing she remembered was the man with the cold, lifeless eyes, who made Keith look like a choir boy, coming up from behind her. "Why'd you run from me, little lamb?" His grating voice asked. And then there was pain. So much pain.

Sky opened her mouth to scream, to demand he leave her alone, but nothing came out. She watched as he lifted his hand, waving two of his fingers in a strange pattern, and then pain pierced her lips. Oh Goddess, what was he doing to her? The feel of a sharp object being stabbed into her flesh, while something weaved in and out, over and over again, hurt like nothing she'd experienced. Before, when Keith had punished her, she'd been able to escape inside her mind, but this man held her with the force of his gaze. Unable to look away or even blink, Sky felt wetness flowing from her eyes and lips, the scent of her own blood filling her senses. Surely, someone would come and rescue her, but the being in front of her only smiled, evil wrapping around them like a cloak.

Minutes that felt more like hours passed, then he laughed. "Much better. You look beautiful now." He held up a mirror allowing Sky to see what he saw. Her face was ghostly white, with streaks of blood pouring from the holes he'd stabbed into her flesh, tracks of tears washing some of it away even as fresh blood oozed. Zigzags of thick black thread weaved back and forth over her mouth, keeping her from opening her lips.

Tears of pain and shame leaked out of her eyes. She was supposed to be a wolf, a predator, but all she'd ever been was the damn prey.

"You have a purpose, little lamb. Keith gifted you some of the Fey powers he stole from Talia. I can feel it pulsing within you. I just need to get you and the stupid bitch in the same place, so she can extract it from you. Then, I will end your sorry excuse of a life. Won't that be wonderful?" His insane laughter scared her almost as much as the loss of her ability to scream or reach out to her alpha through her mind.

She stared at the crazy man in front of her, hating him, hating her life, wishing he would just kill her and be done with it.

"I have no plans to kill you just yet, little lamb, but never fear, your death will come sooner rather than later."

Sky glared at the bastard wishing with all her might he would die a horrible death. The next thing she knew, everything went black.

River and Raydon burst through the woods, coming to a stop a few feet from a man they'd never seen before, growls bursting from them both at the scent of Sky's blood surrounding the area. Their hackles rose as the man raised his free hand, a ball floating above him.

"Back off, mutts, or I'll end your worthless existence along with this one." His hand wavered over the head of Sky.

Sky's fear was palpable, but her unique scent triggered a primal need to claim her through Raydon and him.

"Sky, are you okay?" Niall asked.

A whimper was his answer, sounding muffled. From their vantage point, the only thing they could see was the top of her head. River wanted to rip the man's arm off as he saw his fingers were wrapped around her long golden tresses. The coppery scent of her blood mixed with the salty tang of her tears was making his wolf and Raydon's hard to control. Reaching out to his alpha, he forced the calmness where there was none out. "*She's our mate, Niall.*"

"Why don't you release the female and face me like a man instead of a pussy like you are," Niall taunted.

Hearing Niall's words had Raydon tensing beside him, but River put his arm out, knowing there had to be a reason for what he was doing.

What he'd expected he wasn't sure, but as the bastard laughed, he was prepared for another comment. However, what they got was worse. So much worse than he was prepared for. Nothing in all his thirty years could've equipped him for the sight of their mate being held in front of a monster. Her mouth crudely sewn shut, with what looked like black yarn, had his wolf roaring in his head. He tried to convey to her that they'd save her, that she'd be okay by looking into her eyes, but they too were wrong. There was no color to them, only great pools of blackness with bloody tears leaking from both. His heart broke right then and there, knowing she was suffering, and neither he nor Raydon had been there for her. While they stood staring, blood flowed from each hole where her lips had been sewn, plus trails of red flowed from her ears. Too much blood for one to lose and still stand, he was sure.

"What did you do to her?" Raydon growled the question, his fingers flexing, claws sprouting out of the tips of his hands.

The anguished growl was echoed within him just as he went to leap forward, his own claws out and ready to render the man in half, he slammed into a wall. The sound of Torq's voice telling them to stop finally registered.

"Don't. It's what he wants. He's feeding off your energy. Look," Torq said as he glared over his shoulder.

River looked to see the bastard standing, his arms out as if he was waiting for an influx of power.

"Niall, get control of them," Torq growled then faced the man who held Sky. "So, you like hurting little girls? Why don't you try stepping into the big boys' playground and see if you can hang with the big dogs, or maybe you prefer staying on the porch with the pups?"

"That doesn't even make sense. Which are you? A man or a dog? Let me answer that. You're all nothing but animals to be used when the need arises. This one has served her purpose." He gave Sky one final look, then tossed her aside, her muffled moan cut off as soon as she hit the ground.

River barely kept his beast leashed, knowing whatever the hell was keeping him and Raydon away from their mate wouldn't hold forever.

Even while the battle raged in front of them, neither he nor Raydon took their eyes off their mate, waiting, praying to the Goddess she'd be okay. Through the barrier, her heartbeat was faint and getting weaker.

"Niall, she's dying," he roared, uncaring who heard him.

The sound of swords clashing, then the yells of 'No' followed by heat had him looking up to see a huge creature flying overhead. River knew he should help his packmates, especially when he felt Torq slipping away, but at the same time, he noticed Sky's breathing and heartrate also slowing, then stopping. He gripped his brothers' shoulder, both pushed against the invisible barrier, wanting to hold her, the female they had yet to claim, at least one time, before she was gone from them forever.

"Ock, what's wrong with her?" Lula the dragon asked, rushing to Sky, the invisible barrier no hindrance to her.

River banged against the force holding him back, his wolf clawing forward at the presence of another predator.

"Female, that's our mate. Don't hurt her," Raydon warned Lula.

Lula being Lula ignored them both as she shifted from dragon to human. She glared at them, then waving her hand, she made the wall disappear. Luckily, he and his twin were fast on their feet and kept themselves from falling face first. He made it to Sky's side first, flinching as he got his first up close glimpse of the damage done to her beautiful face. "Stay with us, Sky," he whispered. He wouldn't care what she looked like as long as she was alive.

"It's too late for that, wolfie," Lula said matter-of-factly.

Raydon roared, the anguished sound shook the trees around them. "No, it can't be."

Lula looked at Sky, then at him and Raydon. "I can save her. Bring her back from the brink, but she'll be changed. Can you handle that, twinsies?"

He nodded, his throat too tight for words.

"So it shall be then," Lula sighed. The words no sooner left her mouth, then she shifted again, sweeping Sky up with one large wing, disappearing before their eyes.

"What the hell did you just agree to, River?"

His brother's whispered words deflated the air in his chest. "The only thing I could, Rye, the only thing I could," he repeated.

Across the way, he glimpsed the rest of his pack, sensed Torq's life-force getting stronger, could hear their banter, but until he knew their mate would be alright, he closed himself off to them.

A swift breeze brought his eyes back to the area above them. Blocking out the moon for a moment was a shadow in a cloudless sky, making him think he was hallucinating. "Goddess, is that Lula?" he asked Raydon.

"I do believe it is, and with her is Sky, but she...she smells different." Raydon moved closer as Lula landed a few feet from them.

"That's rude, wolfie." Lula's eyes sparkled as she met theirs. She landed with the grace only she could perform while holding a sleeping Sky tucked close to her chest. "Now, I know you agreed you'd be fine with me being the magnificent dragon I am, but you must promise to not freak out and go all crazy on me, or I'll be forced to kick your wolf butts. That would upset Jenna, and I'd like to avoid doing that."

River didn't waiver. Lula might confuse others, but he understood what she was saying, what her comments were, and he wouldn't go back and change a damn thing. Sky was alive and that was all that mattered to him. He moved forward, his hands itching to take Sky from the huge dragon. "I never go back on my word, dragon."

Before he could take Sky, Lula became a gorgeous human with long pink hair cradling an unconscious Sky in her arms. "I knew that, wolfie. Your female with the strange name is going to be fine. As a matter of fact, the three of you together have quite the weird names. Sky like above us, which is filled with infinite possibilities, River, which can be very deep and murky, and Raydon the protector. Hmm, something to think about. Anyhoo, your mate to be is changed, but not dead. I call that winning. Now, where would you three like to go?"

The only place he wanted to be when Sky woke was at his and Raydon's home. They'd deal with her family later and what their names might mean for their future. He, like all mystical beings, believed there was a reason for everything. The way Lula said their names with such ease and added the little tidbit to each had made him pause for a moment. For now, he and his brother would watch over Sky and help her through whatever changes there was. "Our home."

Lula nodded, then he, Raydon, and Sky were inside their home with Lula standing in front of his large bed where she'd put Sky. "Let her wake on her own. Until then, you can take turns watching over her. I suggest she not be left alone and just be prepared for her to need space. I'll be around if you need me, hopefully."

With that, the female disappeared.

"River, what does she mean, changed? She's said that a couple times, but she looks just the same. Well, she looks better than she did before that bastard got ahold of her. It's as if nothing ever marred her skin." His brother's voice broke, his hand shook as he raised it over Skys head, then pulled back.

"Lula obviously healed her injuries. Maybe there were more internal wounds we didn't see. I don't know, and I don't care. Her scent is the same, only slightly different. I can smell a hint of cotton candy which reminds me of Lula, but that could be because she was with the dragon for however long in the other realm. Shit, we should've asked that question." He raked his hand through his hair, watching as his twin did the same. "She's still ours. I sense her wolf calling to mine. Don't you?" River asked and then went to the opposite side of the bed, leaning down to pull the blanket over Sky. He wasn't as tentative to touch Sky as his brother.

Raydon's breath escaped in a rush. "My wolf wants to mark her now. Clearly, that hasn't changed."

River nodded. "Let's just take care of our mate, and when she wakes up, we'll do whatever it takes to make her realize she belongs with us."

His brother laughed. "Thank the goddess we still have that chance."

"No, thank Lula." The sweet scent of cotton candy still filled the air. Yeah, the pink dragon may be a little weird, but she'd saved their mate, and for that, he'd forever be in her debt.

Raydon watched his brother cover Sky, his chest swelling with love and respect for his twin. If Sky had died, he knew without a doubt, he and River would've followed.

His ears picked up on conversations outside as if they were right next to him. While River and he were almost identical in looks, they had a few things that separated them. One of those was his ability to hear a pin drop, if he was listening for it, even if it was miles away. Of course, he had to know and be focused on that certain pin. Now, he was hyperaware of the dragon, needing to know if there was anything amiss with her or their future mate. Not many knew of his ability outside of his twin and his alpha, since it tended to freak people out. Raydon didn't go around listening in on people's convos for shits and giggles. In all honesty, it was more of a burden as a kid than a thing to celebrate, until now. Turning his head, he allowed his mind to search for the dragon female, pushing aside all other sounds except the one he wanted to hear. Through the long tunnel in his mind, he pushed aside the sounds coming from the woodland creatures, the noise of the forest as the wind blew the trees, everything, until he found Lula.

"*Lord love a duck; do I have to do everything?*" Lula asked.

"*You are the mighty dragon, Lula dear.*" Talia, mate to Torq's voice held a joking note he couldn't miss.

Lula growled; the noise made a wave in his mind, almost pushing him out of the tunnel he was listening through. "*Fine. Off you all go to your beds. I'll even make sure you're nekkid when you get there. Ps. You're welcome.*"

The sounds of his friends' squeals and laughter were cut off, and then he heard several of them expressing their gratitude. "*Thank you, Lula,*" Talia yelled.

"*I love that dragon,*" Torq said.

Raydon wasn't sure if he loved the dragon, but he was grateful they'd have a chance with their mate because of her. Now, they just had to wait and see exactly how Sky was changed and pray to the Goddess she wouldn't be too upset.

"Shit, what about her parents?"

Raydon snapped the link to Lula shut as River's question made him blink. "Fuck, I didn't think of them. Hell, for that matter, do we even know a thing about them?"

River shrugged. "Let's wait till morning. Hopefully, Sky will be awake by then, and can help us decide."

He snorted. "Damn, you already whipped or what?"

"If by whipped you mean I'm willing to allow our mate to decide on what we tell her parents then...what was that?" River held his hand to his ear.

Raydon rolled his eyes and waited.

"Oh, yeah, that was the sound of a whip cracking 'cause yep, I'm whipped. Thank you ma'am, may I have another." River made the sound of a whip cracking, smiling, then sobered as his eyes landed on the silent form of Sky. "For her, I'd do just about anything, Rye."

He and River both took up positions in the huge master bedroom, one on each side of Sky, in chairs not meant to be slept in, but neither were willing to go far. The link he'd forged with the dragon alerted him to her presence, yet he was aware she wasn't speaking to him. His eyes snapped open while his mind followed the path of her voice.

"Female, quit ogling your male and come outside," Lula demanded.

"It's strange how there's only one sun and one moon here, yet I feel as if they're full of magic, you know?" He heard the loneliness in her tone.

Finally the other person spoke, not entirely shocking to him, yet he wondered why Lula went in search of Talia instead of him. *"Yes, it does."*

"The female, Sky, which is a strange name for a human or other, but that's not the point. Anyway, she's going to be a little changed after tonight, and not just because of he who we will not mention, unless you want to mention him because I'm that awesome. Ps. You're welcome." Raydon wanted to reach through the link, shake the female, and demand she tell him everything. Only knowing it would be useless kept him in the chair. Hell, she'd kick his ass and make him say 'Thank you ma'am may I have another,' before burning him to ashes.

"Um, thank you. But, can you elaborate on how Sky will be different? Will I need to explain things to her or the pack?" Talia's hesitant words made him hold his breath.

"Well, it's like this. I'm a very big dragon, and I have lots of dragon to go around, ya know. So, she was sort of dying, and I could see that would've gutted those twin fellas, so I sort of gifted her with some of me. Well, she was already a wolfie, so I'm not really sure what she's gonna be. But, yeah, she's gonna be a little different." There was no worry or fear in Lula's confident words. No, the dragon did what she did, no questions asked.

Silence descended. *"Honey, have you any clue what you've done?"*

Lula growled, the reverberation gave Raydon chills. *"Of course, I know what I did. I'm not a child, Talia Taluleth of the House of Talu. You may be decades old, but I'm centuries older. What I did, I did because she's going to be needed in the future. Now, take your Fey ass back to your mate. He's stirring, and I don't feel like keeping him asleep any longer."*

"*Lula, wait. I didn't mean to offend you. I know you wouldn't do anything to harm someone. But, and this is huge—you giving a piece of yourself away weakens you until you mate."*

Raydon looked at a sleeping Sky, then imagined the great dragon being weak. No, he wouldn't allow either of them to be hurt ever again.

"*Like I said, I have a lot of me to go around. No need to worry. I'll be right as rain. Besides, I don't have a mate. Listen, I got to go. Take care of Sky of the weird name,"* Lula said with a flippant tone that Raydon didn't quite buy.

Before the link to the dragon was severed, he heard Talia's whispered cry. "*Oh, Lula, what have you done?"*

Whatever she'd done, he and River would protect them both. They'd make for damn sure her sacrifice wasn't in vain.

Chapter Two

Sky blinked, trying to bring the room into focus, wondering where she was. "Where am I?" Her voice was a raspy whisper as if she'd gone too long without liquid or she'd gargled glass for shits and giggles.

"You're at our place. Can I get you a drink?"

The voice was one she recognized, the deep baritone belonging to one of two men. Twins who were identical in every way. Her mind felt foggy, her eyes felt as if she'd been in a sand fight. "Why am I here, and for fuckssake, what the hell is going on?" She blinked several times, trying to bring them into focus. "Did I get hit in the head or—that man." Her mind began to race. Images of being tied to a chair, her mouth sewn shut as pain seared her with each needle poke. She reached up, touching her lips, feeling for scars.

"You're okay. You're safe, Sky." The other male with an identical voice spoke up from the other side of the room.

"Why can't I see you clearly? Am I blind? Oh, dear Goddess, did he...he, do something to me?" Panic had her scooting farther away from the voices until her back hit a wall.

"Sweetheart, it's me, Talia. Do you remember me?"

She shook her head back and forth, then nodded, tugging her legs up to her chest. "I want to go home. Please, let me go home."

The sound of more voices entered the small space. How she knew it was small, she didn't know. The echoing sounds made her feel as if the room were no bigger than a cell. They had her in a cell. Did they lock her in. Were they with the man who'd taken her?

"Sky, stop that shit, and stop it now." Her friend Taryn's voice broke through her thoughts.

"Taryn, where are you?" She held out her hand, batting at air.

"Right here. You're going to be fine," Taryn promised.

"Stop saying that. Everyone just stop fucking saying that. I can't see. What happened to my eyes?"

Silence descended. She counted seven people in the room by their heartbeats. All were breathing hard, and her friend Taryn was crying. "Stop fucking crying, Taryn. Just tell me what happened and don't sugar coat it. I watched you be broken from the inside out. I had to wash the blood and gore from your body more than once. I even had to wipe your ass, so don't you dare try to sugar coat this." Her voice trembled, but she didn't care.

When she thought nobody was going to answer her, she prepared to get up and—what she'd do she didn't know. Hell, she couldn't whoop her way out of a wet paper bag, let alone walk out of wherever the hell she was with dignity.

"Right now, you appear to have a cloudy substance over your eyes, but they're clearer today than they were yesterday." Taryn paused. "Every day, they're a little better. We just don't know. It's not like we've come across this before."

"How long have I been here?"

Again, the silence was deafening. "Fucking answer me, or get the hell away, so I can make my way out of here. Someone will tell me." Her parents would, probably.

"Two weeks, hellmouth."

"River, don't."

"No, let him speak. At least he's being honest." She was shocked at the amount of time she'd been out of it and tried not to let it show, but it was hard, especially with her emotions so raw.

"Now that you're awake, I can try to heal you, if you agree." Talia's voice was even. Goddess, being unable to see, she was picking up on every other nuance of things. Next, she'd be counting breaths, knowing who was skipping one. Fuck. That.

"Let's do it, Fey." She took a deep inhale of air, nearly choking on everyone else's fear.

"Wait, what are the consequences?" River asked.

"The consequences are I'll be fucking blind, and if you keep putting your two cents in, you're going to get your nuts smacked," she warned. River wanted to call her hellmouth, she'd show him hellmouth.

"Hellmouth, keep it up, and I'll put you over my lap and teach you some manners," River growled.

"How about everyone clear out while I see what I can do for Sky?" Didn't Talia the broken Fey sound so damn reasonable.

"Be nice, or my reasonable mate will leave your ass to whatever your fate has in store for you, Sky," Torq growled.

Shit, she didn't realize she'd said that out loud. Goddess, she just wanted to rewind time and go back to before. Before they left the compound. No. That wasn't true. At the compound her best friend was being abused by her crazy dad while she too had to suffer, in silence, almost the exact same fate. Oh, and let's not forget her best friend's mom, the woman who was now offering to heal her was being held captive in a cell. But dammit, her life really sucked since then, too.

The number of heartbeats went down. She assumed it was her, Talia, and Talia's mate.

"Alright, hellmouth, you keep your cool and just do what Talia says. You got a lot of people surrounding you with good vibes and shit."

Well shit, she sucked.

As far as devotions go, River really sort of sucked at them, but no shifter wanted to mate up with a blind female.

"I'm ready when you are, Talia." She tried to sound confident but having no clue what was going to happen was really putting a damper on her confidence.

"Sky, if you begin to feel any pain, let me know. I'm going to place my hands on either side of your head," Talia paused, then touched Sky on each of her temples.

She walked Sky through what she was going to do, explaining step by step the process, but to Sky it wouldn't matter as long as the end game was her seeing again.

Time slipped away while Talia worked slowly, methodically. Sky let herself float away while the other woman worked. Her mind reached for River's and Raydon's, slipping inside theirs without alerting them. They were alike, yet different. She didn't stay long, only skimming the surface. An exclamation had her blinking to see Talia kneeling in front of her on the bed, her body shaking.

"It's really bright in here," Sky sobbed, wrapping her arms around Talia, her cries soaking into the other woman's shirt. She hid her face, not wanting to show weakness to the others.

"Does it hurt?" Talia asked.

Sky raised her head, looking over at River, who stood by the door, a shocked expression on his face. Raydon eased inside, his face a study in worry like they'd both aged a few years in the last couple weeks. "What's wrong with you both?" They were freaking Sky out.

"Nothing, we feared you were never going to wake up, and then when you couldn't see...we're relieved," River said, truth ringing out in his every word.

"Now answer the question. Are you hurting?" Raydon strolled toward the bed, not stopping until he was within touching distance.

"No, I just thought I was never going to see light again. I know it sounds stupid 'cause it's only been whatever, but oh goddess, it was so scary. You don't know," she cried.

Talia let her cry, acting more like a mother than Sky's had ever done. Heck, she wondered where her parents were. If she'd been out for weeks, had they called her parents? "Did anyone call my parents?" she had to ask even knowing they probably had and hated the fact others would know how little they cared. Niall being their alpha now would've made sure they were aware.

The growl from the other room had her turning toward the door. "What the hell is that?"

"How's everything going?" Taryn asked, pulling her attention away from the strange noise.

"I'm crying like a whiny ass bitch. How's it look like it's going?" Sky asked, raising her face, realizing nobody answered her. In all honesty, she didn't care either way. She had money secured away that neither of her parents could touch. Once she was able to stand on her own without falling over, she'd...do what had to be done.

Taryn gasped, then wrapped her arms around Sky. "Don't you ever do that to me again."

Talia eased off the bed, nearly falling on her ass when her feet hit the floor. "I got you, farfalla. Come on, let's give them some time." Torq's deep baritone rumbled around them.

"Oh goddess, are you alright? What's wrong with her?" Sky scrambled up after Talia.

Torq turned with his mate in his arms. "She just needs to rest after healing you. Don't..." he shook his head, stopping Sky. "She would never have allowed you to suffer if she could help, which is what she did."

They left the room, shutting the door behind them, leaving her alone with Taryn. Her senses flared, picking up conversations she shouldn't be able to, hearing animals too far away, making her hyper-aware something was very different about her.

Sky listened as Talia accepted water from Cora, the second to the pack alpha's mate and also a veterinarian. To hear the powerful Fey woman's voice shaking as she accepted the glass of water made the guilt even worse for Sky.

"*Thank you, Cora. Um, I made all the medical equipment disappear. If you need it, I can get you more,*" Talia said to Cora.

"*I appreciate that. Who knows when I'll need it again.*" Cora cleared her throat.

"*Her eyes are purple. Not like the light hit them and they looked purple, but they're fucking purple. Like the dragon female's,*" River announced. His voice angry.

Sky bit her lip, worrying over what others would think of her changes.

Lula's words and memories slammed into her. She'd given her a sliver of herself, nothing major the pink dragon had said, just enough to keep her from being...well, dead. What else was different, other than her eyes were now purple, and she could hear every fucking thing like it was amplified? Goddess, the saying if a tree fell in the woods, would anyone hear it? Yes. Yes, she'd fucking hear it, motherfuckingsonofabitch. She felt a pulse of magic and more talking from outside the room while she tried to filter out the noise she didn't want to hear. Twin growls had her girlie parts quivering. What the hell was wrong with her? She did not quiver, damn her traitorous body.

Once she stopped worrying so much as to whether trees cried, she could see the pulse of magic. "I'll be damned," she muttered. "You won't hide shit from me," she snarled, her wolf rising from her slumber inside her.

"What the hell are you talking about?" Taryn asked.

Sky pointed toward the door. "Do you not see that, or feel it?"

Taryn looked where Sky pointed. "Sorry, but no. Maybe you should lay back down. Maybe I should call Talia or Peyton back in here." Her voice rose in clear panic.

With a raise of her hand, Sky waved Taryn's suggestions away. "The hell. I don't need to rest anymore than I have. Two damn weeks is long enough, don't you think?"

"You've really developed a potty mouth. I like it," Taryn laughed.

"I was on Fey for well over a month with a crazy pink dragon. I think she wore off on me."

Her words had Taryn gasping. "A month?"

Before she had to explain what that month entailed, she headed for the door.

"So, what you're saying is, that in order to save her, Lula put a dragon...in her?" Niall asked.

"I really don't know, and neither did Lula. Only time will tell. But one thing that is for sure, is her eyes are that of Lula's." Talia sighed.

Sky walked out of the room with a puzzled Taryn trailing her. "Newsflash, your bubble doesn't work on me. Clearly, that's something dragonish I've got. So, I have purple eyes, and I might be a fucking dragonwolf. Great. Sign me up for freak of the fucking week."

"Hellmouth, I'll put you over my knee," River warned.

Raydon tilted his head back. "Goddess give me strength."

Torq clapped his hands. "Alright, folks, looks like our job here is done. I'm taking my Fey mate home and try to talk her into making babies."

Taryn groaned. "Oh lord I didn't need to hear that. Sky, burn me with your laser eyes."

Sky slapped at Taryn. "That's so not funny, beotch."

"And hearing your mom is going to go bump uglies with her mate isn't either." Taryn gagged.

Stifling her laughter, Sky met Talia's gaze. "Thank you for what you did for me." She pointed toward her eyes.

Talia walked up to her with Torq. "I'm here if you need anything or have any questions."

At that moment she just wanted everyone gone so she could process.

"Alright, party's over. Everyone, out." River pointed toward the door.

Bronx clapped his hands together. "That's our cue." He and Taya stood by the fireplace, rising gracefully.

"When you get done figuring shit out, get in touch. We'll handle you and Raydon's shifts at Chaps and Garage Inc until." Bronx looked at Raydon and then River. "Well, until your shit is settled."

Jett straightened from the far wall, his hand raising. Sky wished she had a connection like her friend Taryn did with Jett. The love was clear to anyone who looked between the two, even though the man had been known as the Magic Mike of the shifter world. Now, the only bumping and grinding would be done with Taryn. "You ready, Taryn?"

"Yeah, just a second. Sky, you need anything, I'm only a holler away." Taryn pointed at her head, then her eyes narrowed. "Why can't I connect with you?"

"Just leave it for now. My head hurts, and I just need to breathe." She closed her eyes, her purple fucking eyes. Goddess, everything was different now.

River could see Sky was struggling to stay civil. Hell, he and his brother were having a hard time keeping their own wolves level, knowing she had a wolf, and possibly a dragon inside her. Neither of them knew what to say with all the new knowledge. One thing was for certain, and that was they wanted some alone time with her.

"You three need anything, you only have to ask. Sky, as your alpha, I'm here for you, but you need to realize this is new for all of us. There's going to be an adjustment period, and I'm aware as is everyone. Be patient but also be honest. Our pack is built on honesty, loyalty, and above all love for one another. That includes you. Talia risked her life for you as would any member of the Mystic Wolves. When you became one of us, you vowed to do the same. It didn't change just because you got caught in the crosshair of a psycho and now you've got a little something extra. Embrace it, and life will even out for you." Niall pulled Sky forward, his blue eyes staring into Sky's. "Welcome back, little one." He kissed her forehead, then stepped back.

Alaina sighed. "See, that's why I love him, and he's so getting lucky tonight."

River was sure he heard Talia say something about neutering, but then he blocked out the others. "Are you thirsty?" he asked.

Sky licked her lips. "I could use something a lot stronger than water."

Raydon grunted. "I'm thinking that wouldn't be very wise."

"Pretty sure you're not my daddy, or the boss of me." Sky faced off with Raydon.

"Enough you two. Raydon, let's all have a drink and settle in the family room. I think we could all use a stiff drink."

He knew one of the reasons his twin was angry at Sky's words. The mention of dad was a reminder that their soon to be mate's parents hadn't shown an ounce of care to their daughter's wellbeing, let alone whether she lived or died. For fuckssake, they'd been more concerned with whether anyone in the pack knew where she kept her bank info. No way in hell would he tell Sky the truth of her parents' lack of interest.

"Alright, what'll it be? We've got beer, wine, and Patron." River glanced over his shoulder from the fridge, catching Sky staring at his ass. Her cheeks turned a sweet pink. He couldn't wait to find out if she blushed all over with the same shade.

"You keep your tequila in the fridge?" she asked with one raised brow.

River opened the stainless-steel door wider. "The freezer for Patron Burdeos. This tequila is aged for at least a year in French and American oak before it finally gets put into the Bordeaux wine casks. You see this?" River held the bottle up with the burnt caramel looking liquid inside. "Once the tequila is ready, the flavor is rich with vanilla and bright with dried fruit, some of the best there is out there." He poured three double shots, then recapped the bottle.

"Ask him how much that lovely tequila costs, hellmouth." Raydon reached for his glass, raising a brow when River moved it out of his reach.

"If you're gonna talk that shit about fine Patron, then you can get the lower shelf tequila." River tilted his head toward the clear bottle of tequila that sat on the counter.

"Alright, I give. What's a bottle of that cost, like fifty dollars?"

River pushed her drink across to her, nudging Raydon's toward him, then taking his own. "How about we drink first, then I'll tell you. Do you like tequila, Sky?"

Sky shrugged. "What're we going to drink to?"

"To the future," Raydon suggested.

"Sounds very promising," Sky agreed. "Bottoms up, boys." She tapped her glass to River's and then Raydon's, swallowing the entire drink in one gulp.

River waited for her to cough, or more likely hack, but she just closed her eyes, her chest rose and fell a couple times, then her bright purple eyes opened. "Damn, I think I like tequila. How much does a bottle like that set a girl back?"

Raydon laughed. "I think it's a little over five hundred. Right, River?"

Tossing his own drink back, he kept his eyes pinned to Sky's, waiting to see how she took the news of the expense. "About that, bro," he agreed.

"Well, I guess I'll need to get me a couple ordered and only share with those I like then. Damn, that's some spendy liquor."

She shocked him with her words. Not only did she not look at him and his brother like they were crazy for spending that amount of cash on alcohol, but she planned to buy some for herself. Of course, neither of them would allow her to shell out that kind of dough. If their mate wanted a few bottles of five hundred dollar tequila just for herself, they'd make damn sure she had it. However, the only people he hoped she planned to share it with were him and Raydon. The fact they still hadn't mentioned the truth about them being fated mates ate at him.

Shit, what if the dragon in her—rejected them?

"You have questions, I can see them written all over your face, but right now, I just want to...be. My wolf is raking at me for freedom. There's this other being inside me. It's a part of me, yet I don't recognize it. Does that even make sense? My world feels like a fucking roller coaster I didn't agree to go on, and right now, I just want to slow down," she sighed. "Can I have another drink, please?" She held her hand out, a slight tremor made the glass shake.

"*She's breaking my fucking heart, Rye. I can't deny her anything, but I want to demand she let us in. I want to hold her and protect her, and promise everything is going to be okay, but fuck, I don't know that everything will be.*" He spoke to his twin through their link, keeping his expression neutral, ensuring Sky wouldn't be aware. The last thing he wanted to do was make her think they were keeping anything from her.

"*You need to just chill. Let's go sit down and get to know her on a regular level.*" Raydon sat his glass down. "Want a refill, or would you prefer something else?" he asked Sky.

Their little mate narrowed her eyes. "I want you both to use your outside voices, and don't do that man speak or whatever twin thing you got going on. I know it's probably instinctual to talk to one another inside your heads, but I'd appreciate it if you didn't do it...all the time." Sky reached for the bottle of Patron and filled her glass. "Sorry if I'm being bitchy, but I feel as if the world has sort of picked me up, spun me around, and dropped me on my head. For you two, it's been two weeks. For me, it's been a little longer, like a month, and things aren't the same as when I left." She slammed her second drink back, closing her eyes while they watched her throat swallow.

River grimaced, thinking she was definitely going to feel the affects of the alcohol if she kept it up. They were shifters, so alcohol didn't usually do to them what it did to humans, which was why he froze the good stuff. While it diluted it for humans, for their kind, it was like doubling the alcohol content for them. Maybe he should've mentioned that to Sky.

"You've nothing to apologize for, hellmouth. Come on, let's go relax and drink more of my brother's finest tequila. Time has no meaning for us, tonight." Raydon lifted Sky into his arms, making her squeal.

"Um, I can walk, you know?" Sky wrapped one arm around his shoulders but didn't protest any more.

Raydon grunted. "Yep," he agreed.

River grabbed his bottle of five hundred dollar tequila and the three glasses, following in the footsteps of the two people who meant the most to him in the world. Tonight, he'd drink, talk, and hopefully learn more about Sky. Tomorrow, they'd make plans for their future.

Chapter Three

Raydon could see his twin was nervous. Hell, he was too, but having Sky in his arms as he carried her into their large great room was a dream come to reality. She was so slight in his embrace, almost too small for them, but the goddess had created her just for them. Fuck, he wasn't sure what the woman who had made them who they were, had planned for them, but taking their mate away, only to return her and tossing in a dragon wolf, wasn't something he'd counted on.

"Yep, you know I can walk, but you're still going to carry me? If you keep this up, I'll forget how to walk all together." Sky nuzzled into his neck.

He tilted his own head down and brushed his nose along the side of her face down to her neck, inhaling the sweet smell of Sky. She still had the syrupy scent of cotton candy, but he also detected what he thought was spiced apples. The combination made his mouth water and his wolf whine for a taste. "Well, if you forget to walk, then it'll be our duty to carry you around, or better yet, keep you in bed until...well, we'll figure it out as we go on." He gave a mock growl as images of what he and his brother could do with their mate if they were in bed together, day in and day out. Fuck, they'd all forget how to walk.

Sky ran her fingers through the back of his hair, giving a slight tug. "I don't think so, mister. I like walking and driving. Besides, have you seen that movie WALL-E where humans didn't walk because, well whatever reason, and subsequently they lost all their muscle mass and ended up being big blobs? Err, not happening."

He stopped in front of the sectional with the lounge section piled high with pillows, staring down at Sky. "Alright, I give. What the hell is WALL-E, and why the fuck did humans stop walking? Do I even want to know how they got around?"

River came up behind them laughing. "Dude, it's a cartoon about a robot named WALL-E. The humans all fled Earth and were in space for like, ever. They motored around on floating wheelchair like things."

Raydon turned and settled himself on the chaise part of the couch with Sky on his lap. Nobody could ever claim he wasn't a good multi-tasker. "And you know this, why?" he asked.

"Nolan has a great collection of kids shows, and that one has an excellent message. Take care of Earth, and it will take care of you." River shrugged, before sitting down with the remote in his hand. "Any requests?" He pulled up their lists of movies for Sky to see, placing her legs on his lap.

Once River started scrolling, Sky settled against his chest, making his wolf rumble inside him. Her heart steadily pounding as his own echoed the same tempo, was something he'd wanted, yet didn't think they'd find.

"I like chick flicks and action movies. How about you guys? Please tell me you don't like horror movies." She held her hand up, fingers crossed.

While River debated the wonders of a good horror film with Sky, he allowed his senses to flare, spreading wider until he was sure there wasn't a threat to them or their little wolf. When he was pulling back, a sense of another being, one that was familiar, yet not quite, tugged at him. The presence, closer than he liked, but then it was gone as if he'd been mistaken.

"What is it?" Sky asked.

Raydon closed his eyes, trying to place exactly what he'd felt and put into words something that would make sense without scaring Sky. He opened his mouth, then closed it, knowing nothing he thought would come out the way it would have felt in his mind. "I was just double checking the perimeter around here, making sure all was clear."

River grunted, drawing Sky's attention. "You'll find there are distinct differences in us. I'm the fun one, while he's the worrier."

Raydon tipped his lips up in a grin, opening his mind to River even as he kept a shield around their thoughts. *"I felt a familiar presence just outside the southside of the cabin. It felt like...Sky, but not Sky. I don't know; it makes no sense, but it was there one minute and then gone. However, you and I both know she hasn't left our laps."* He ran his hand down Sky's arm, his gesture both physical and mental. No way in hell had their female been anywhere other than right where she was. With them.

"Maybe you're feeling a residual presence from when she'd been here from before?" River rubbed one of Sky's insteps, making her sigh.

Neither of them believed that, but they both fell silent.

"No matter what the hell it was, she's not to be out of our sights. Agreed?" Raydon gathered Sky closer, needing to feel her heat, to know she was safe.

"You know when you guys do your twin speak, I told you I can feel it. It's like this current is passing between you, but there's a wall that's almost visible. It's rude, ya know," she said, not taking her eyes away from the big screen television.

River growled, pulling her from Raydon. "You can feel it when we speak to one another?"

A slight lift of her shoulder was his answer.

Raydon wanted to take Sky back from his twin, her words and the hurt radiating from her made him and his wolf edgy. "We're sorry, Sky. We've always spoke between one another in the same way, without thought."

Sky nodded, looking from River to Raydon. "I get that, but I have a feeling I was the topic of conversation, which makes it rude. If you two are going to talk about me, I'd appreciate it if you'd do so out loud or include me in the conversation link."

Her words made him feel like an asshole. He couldn't promise to always include her, not if her safety was in question, or that of the pack's security. Fuck, how did other males handle situations like this?

"How about a compromise? We promise to include you, unless it's detrimental to the safety of you or others?"

Their little female's eyes narrowed, warning them she was thinking. Her chest rose and fell while she took deep breaths in and out. "Fine, but just so you both are aware, that goes three ways. If I feel shit needs to be kept from the both of you, then I guess I'll do it."

River's eyes flashed, a clear sign he was close to losing his temper.

"Hellmouth, you can't expect two alpha males to accept those terms," Raydon muttered, getting up from the couch. When he was angry, he tended to pace while River tended to lash out.

Sky scrambled up from her perch on River's lap. "I'm gonna need you both to listen and listen very carefully. This is all new to me. Having gone from an... asshole alpha like Keith, to what I just went through, to becoming whatever the hell I am now. I need to know that I'm an equal, not some little female you tuck away until you deem it's acceptable to do whatever the fuck you think is okay."

Raydon moved in front of her, putting his hands on her shoulders. Electricity sparked from her to him. "We'd never think to do that to you. Sky, for a true male of worth, it's second nature to want to protect their female. What you were brought up around, that bastard who called himself your alpha, was nothing like what a real alpha is like. For us, for all the males in our pack, it's written in our DNA to shield those who are," he paused at the heated glare in Sky's eyes. "Fuck, I don't want to sound condescending, but dammit, most females are more than happy to be protected. I know you're fearsome and shit, what with having part of a dragon in you. That's a learning curve we all need to come to terms with. For us, we've been taught that women are to be protected above all others. Mates are to be placed above all others. For us, that makes you our top priority as not only our mate, but our female."

Sky could see Raydon and River both felt immense longing to soothe her. On one side, her wolf wanted to let them both in, but the other side, the one with the dragon wanted to prove she could protect herself and their young. Whoa, slow your roll dragon chick. No way was she ready to have young with the two sexy twins. Her heart and body may be ready, but her mind wasn't.

"I know what you're saying is true. I do. It's just hard to break a lifetime of teaching in a few short months. Toss in this." She circled her face, knowing they'd understand her own big change didn't just encompass the fact she now sported purple eyes, but everything. At least she hoped they would. "The truth is, I don't have a clue what's going to happen tomorrow, and neither do you. When I was in the Fey Realm, I would've happily stayed there. Don't growl. There was no pain, no pressure, nothing. I was free of everything. There was so much peace. Now, I have all these feelings and insecurities. I need to know I can trust you both to be honest with me and trust that I can handle whatever comes our way. If you're going to treat me like the little female who needs to be tucked away while the big bad men take care of shit, then we are going to have major problems."

River turned her to face him. "Sky, we can promise to try our best, but we will be breaking a lifetime of conditioning. Can you give us a chance for all of us to work through this together?"

Looking from one man to the other, she could tell they truly meant it. For her, they'd both try to be what she needed. Could she do the same? "I think time is something we all have in spades," she agreed.

Raydon's breath feathered over her shoulder, his warmth at her back reminded her of what else these two men would expect from her. "We move at your pace, Sky."

"So, if I tell you that I'm not ready to be with you both?" She bit her lip, waiting without opening her senses.

River's thumb pressed against her mouth, removing her lip from between her teeth. "You need time, you got it. You need space, although it would gut us, you got it."

Raydon wrapped his arms around her from behind. "We can all share a bed and not do anything other than hold you, love."

Sky snorted, looking over her shoulder at Raydon. "Do you really believe that?" She wasn't a virgin, yet she was far from a whore. However, laying in a bed with the two men would be nearly impossible for her not to want to do more than just sleep. A yawn escaped her, sending a shiver down her spine.

"Come on, hellmouth. I'll show you where you'll sleep. River and I'll sleep in the guest rooms." Raydon swung her up in his arms, not giving her a chance to agree or protest. Of course, she enjoyed being in both of the twins arms a little too much, which was something she'd keep to herself.

Inside the bedroom he took her to, she swore they'd read her mind, or had somehow gotten a hold of her fantasy dream bedroom. The super-sized bed was larger than any she'd ever seen, yet if it was going to be a bed made for three grown adults, it was perfect. The elegant room was something she'd not expected either man to have designed. "This is beautiful," she breathed.

The four-poster bed in a dark wood piled high with soft grey fabric and more white pillows than she could count beckoned to her. She wiggled to get down, wanting to touch it to make sure it was real. As soon as her feet touched the cool hardwood, she quickly crossed the room, her feet delighting in the mixture of textures as they stepped onto the huge rug at the end of the bed. "Who picked all this out?" She gestured toward the dark grey rug she stood on, then at the blush colored accents around the room.

River cleared his throat. "Well, it was kind of a combined effort."

She dug her toes into the faux fur beneath her, then walked around to the side of the bed, her hand trailing over the fabric. "I know I should ask more questions, but right now, I can't think of one." Her jaw cracked as another yawn escaped her.

Raydon came back into the room from a door near the side table, the sound of water running drew her attention. "I started you a bath. It'll help you relax and make you sleep better."

Again, she pulled her bottom lip into her mouth, indecision warring within her. "I think a quick shower will suffice."

"River and I'll wait out here for you. Take a bath and relax. If you need anything, holler, hellmouth. You're safer here, right this minute, than anywhere on Earth."

Her body ached to be touched, but her mind said no way hussy. She took a step away from the comfy looking bed, then another, until she was in the doorway where the water was louder. She knew the bathroom was going to be just as opulent as the bedroom, with all the touches she'd have put in it. How she knew, she didn't know, but for a second, she closed her eyes before turning to face her dream bath. A small gasp escaped as she saw for the first time the spa like bathroom with the huge clawfoot tub in the center of the space. It was done in a color scheme that matched the bedroom. Towels that looked large enough to cover both men were perfectly rolled and placed on the counter where candles were burning. However, there was already one set out for her. "This is beautiful and perfect, and I think I'm going to cry," she whispered, knowing both men would hear her.

"Everything you need is right there," River said, pointing toward the bath tub that was filling up. The shelf had all her favorites, from body wash, shampoo, and conditioner to the lotion she preferred. "If you need any assistance, let us know." The heat that flared from him let Sky know he was more than up for the challenge.

"I'll be fine, thanks." She smiled, then gave a small wave of her hand waiting until they left before she quickly stripped and eased into the warm water. "Damn. Perfect," she swore.

Even through the door she could feel their pleasure in her own. Her wolf was ready to let the twins claim her, but Sky needed more than a day, or rather night, to accept all the changes. It didn't matter that she'd been away in a different realm for over a month, or in a coma like state here for over two weeks while they watched over her. No, she needed to...be here and present for a while. Time to get to truly know them, and her new self. A damn dragon was inside her, taking up space with her wolf. Although, to be truthful, Sky didn't feel the dragon bit, neither did her wolf. "Let it go," she whispered out loud, hoping the words would resonate inside her mind as well.

After she washed and rinsed her hair several times, she finally got out, drying off quickly. A scan of the area showed no sign of pajamas, not that she was a fan of anything formal. She was a shorts and a tank top girl, and she was good to go, but a girl needed something on around Raydon and River, or she was sure to find herself in a compromising position, or ten. The image of a couple of those positions were enough to make her body go liquid, which was so not what she needed. Not when the men in question were right outside the door and would be able to smell her need. To get her mind out of the gutter, she thought of her old life, which didn't hold many happy memories.

"Hellmouth, you okay in there?" Raydon asked.

The deep timber had her pulling back from the memories. "I'm fine. Do you...ah, do you have something I can wear?"

A growl followed by another sent a shiver of awareness down her spine. "Stop it, you hussy," she told herself.

One loud knock was her warning before the door was pushed open, then entered River with a black T-shirt in his right fist. "You can wear one of my shirts. It'll be big enough to be more like a dress, then tomorrow we can swing by the cabin and grab some of your things."

She raised her right brow, wondering why they assumed she'd be moving in with them. Of course, it was what she wanted and planned...eventually. Her wolf rolled onto her back, all four legs in the air, damn hussy. Sky ignored her, focusing on the black material. "Thanks." When her fingers touched his, a spark flew between them, making her jump. "Oh," she exclaimed. "Did you feel that?"

River nodded. "It's happened each time we've touched you. Usually, it settles after a couple seconds of contact."

To make his point, he placed his other hand on top of hers, the zing of electricity arced again, then became a low hum before fading. Her eyes sought Raydon's, seeing his nod as if he understood her unspoken question.

"I slept through these jolts?" She couldn't keep the marvel out of her tone. The little zaps were like being shocked by static electricity.

"It would seem so. While you slept, you didn't appear to be aware of anything that happened. Neither Rye or I left you alone, without one of us with you."

Why hearing she'd been watched over by the two gorgeous men didn't make her run for the hills was something she'd examine later. After she had some sleep that wasn't coma induced. "Thank you, the both of you. I really just want to sleep of my own volition. Wake when I want and feel refreshed after a few hours, not weeks." She held the towel with one hand, the other held out for the black T-shirt.

Raydon filled the doorway, both arms braced on the frame above his head. "We can give you space, hellmouth. Whatever it is you need, you have only to ask."

She pulled the black material to her chest, keeping from burying her nose in it by sheer will. Her wolf stood inside her head, making Sky aware she was drooping. "You'd think I'd be alert and ready to face the world or at least not quite so tired." She covered her mouth, trying to stifle another yawn.

"Get dressed and come on out when you're finished," River ordered.

Sky tilted her head to the side. "Yes, sir. Anything else, sir?" she grinned.

He pointed one big finger at her. "Keep sassing me and you'll find out what else, hellmouth."

She pointed her finger at him, mimicking his stance. "Out, so I can get dressed. You don't want me to fry you with my laser eyes, do you?"

Raydon took two steps into the room. "There's a lot we want you to do, but frying us, sure as shit ain't one of them, love." Before she could say a word, he covered her lips with his, giving her a quick hard kiss, then turned and left, hollering for River over his shoulder.

"He's bossy," River said. He then tugged Sky toward him, sipping at her lips as if he had all the time in the world, before he too stepped back, looking at her with an intensity that she could feel like a living breathing thing.

Her lips tingled from the dual kisses, choking her up. All she really knew about the twins were they called to her and her wolf. But she was different now. Would they still want her if they knew just how different she was? She went to the mirror, looking at herself, checking for changes. Her fingers traced her lips, the feel of the imaginary needle going in and out made her wince. She looked closer, checking for the holes, looking for scars. "Amazing," she whispered. She pulled her top lip away from her teeth, pinching the flesh. Nothing. No sign of the damage she knew had been there. Goddess, how she wished it hadn't been so. Yes, she'd been given the option of her memories wiped, but that wouldn't have been right. She wanted to remember. Nothing in life was ever gained by forgetting. However, standing there staring at herself, yet not recognizing the person looking back, Sky wasn't so sure she'd made the right decision.

After she brushed her teeth with the toothbrush she found in the cabinet, new, next to theirs, she brushed her hair out, and pulled it into a top knot before pulling the T-shirt on. "Time to face the wolves," she snorted at her words. As she stepped out of the bathroom, she was surprised to find both men no where in sight. Their scents still lingered, but they'd given her space. Oh, she knew they were within yelling distance, but clearly, they were intelligent enough to know she needed space. Why then did her heart ache at their absence. "Because I'm a silly girl," she mumbled.

The big bed looked too big for one, but Sky wouldn't be that female who would flip flop on her declarations. She'd asked for time and space, and they gave it. One of them had pulled back the corner of the comforter, exposing the sheets beneath. With a deep sigh, she climbed up and snuggled beneath what could only be described as utter opulence. Seriously, they must've spent a fortune on the bedding.

Sky closed her eyes, her mind settled with the comforting sounds of River and Raydon moving around in the rooms outside of the bedroom. She pictured them preparing for bed, their scents invading her senses, soothing all her ragged edges. A sigh escaped as her eyes drifted closed, absolute rightness making it easy for her to relax and let go.

"It's about time. I've been waiting on you forever."

Sky jolted at the familiar voice, spinning to face who'd spoken. Her hand went to her chest, covering her heart. "Who are you?"

The female smiled, her blue eyes flickered black then blue again. "Why, I'm you of course. Or your twin, I should say."

She shook her head. "I don't have a twin." Her heart raced beneath her palm as the look alike moved toward her. They were standing in a space that Sky could only describe as a black void. Nothing looked familiar. There was no scent, no color, just them and then...nothing. "Where are we?"

"We are in the void. It's where I've been since birth. Only, I wasn't born, you were. Now, though, I have a chance thanks to circumstances. We're what's called Chimera Twins." The female moved closer, her aura a dark swirl around her.

"No, I would've felt you. My mother would've said something if I'd been a twin." Sky was sure of it, if for no other reason than to dig at Sky for being unworthy.

The Chimera shook her head. "Mother was ashamed she couldn't carry both of us. It was actually your fault, you know. You took too much and wouldn't allow me to grow."

Sky wasn't sure what was or wasn't. Her mind tried to pull up her knowledge on Chimera twins, but a fog blocked her. Her wolf whined.

"Ah and your wolf wouldn't allow you to share either, but all that will change. Now that you have twin mates, you need me. You're not a female who can handle two males such as the two who want you. How long do you think they'll stay faithful to a little mouse such as yourself, hmm?" She circled Sky, her body moving sinuously. "You're lack of—experience will turn them off, while I've had more than enough in the other realms, to entice and keep them both satisfied. You won't have to worry they'll leave and find another. Together, we can keep our mates satisfied."

A shard of jealousy stabbed her. They were not *their* mates, but her mates. "I don't know who or what you are, but you're not my twin, Chimera or not. Raydon and River are mine, and I'll have no problem keeping them happy."

The female was closer than Sky had realized, her long nails looking like daggers, raised. "Ah, you poor naïve soul. You think you have a choice." One long nail raked across Sky's cheek. The sharp pain making her cry out. "I will continue to get stronger until I will be the only one in this body." The fingernail raked along her neck, stopping above Sky's hand where it rested above her heart. "Your heart that beats will be my heart. You've had this body for the last twenty-five years. It's my turn. If you don't want to share, then I'll take over completely. Your men won't even notice when you're gone, and it's me they're fucking. Hell, they'll probably enjoy it more since I don't think missionary is the only way, poppet."

The thought of the other female seducing her men had her seeing red. "Over my dead body, bitch."

The Chimera laughed, sounding nothing like Sky, yet she looked like Sky. It was freaking her out.

"Oh, sweet little, Sky, don't you get it? You won't have a choice in the matter." A sharp pain stabbed Sky and then she was alone in the darkness.

She gasped, fighting to wake up, her hand going to her chest. Shivers wracked her while she tried to get air in her lungs. The sound of feet slapping hardwood heralded the arrival of first River then Raydon, both men hurrying into the room, their eyes scanning every corner as if they thought there was a threat. Little did they know the threat was inside of her.

"Are you okay? Why'd you scream?" River fired the questions out one after the other.

Sky pulled herself into a sitting position, taking the comforter with her until her back hit the headboard. "I...I had a nightmare." What could she tell them, that she'd dreamt she had a twin and that twin was batshitcrazy? Nope, not today.

Raydon nodded, sitting down next to her hip. His hand brushed the hair off her forehead that had escaped from her messy bun. "You think you can go back to sleep, or you want to come into the kitchen for some breakfast?"

By the way the glimmer of light came in the window, she estimated the time to be around five in the morning. Much earlier than she normally would get up, but not like it was the ass-crack of dawn. "Let me go to the bathroom and then I'll meet you in the kitchen."

River leaned down, kissing her forehead. "You sleep with one or both of us, and we'll chase away all your nightmares."

"Oh really? How you gonna do that?" she asked with a laugh.

With his face an inch from hers, she could smell the minty hint of his toothpaste. "Because we'd leave you so exhausted you wouldn't have the strength to dream, let alone have a nightmare."

His words conjured up all kinds of images, but in the end, she was too keyed up from what had been in her dreams. Now that she was awake, she didn't think it was actually real, more like a nightmare. Her mind making up things that somehow twisted reality in dreams. If she only knew how to interpret them. Maybe she'd buy one of those dream interpretation books and find out what it meant to see yourself as a twin in your dreams. Surely, she wasn't the only person to have ever dreamt such dreams. Undoubtedly, others had to have felt as if there truly was another being living inside of them. A different person altogether, one who was her, but not?

Chapter Four

River didn't know what had put that look of fear in Sky's eyes, but whatever, or whoever, would pay dearly when he and Raydon found them. They'd begun to wonder if there was a female out there for them when they'd gotten a whiff of the elusive young female's scent. From that point on, he'd known she was it. It had taken very little suggestion to get Raydon to agree. Now, it seemed he and Raydon were both on the same page. Protect, honor, and love one wicked little wolf. The long wait for her to wake and recover had nearly driven them both crazy, only the reassurance she was getting better from Emerson and Peyton kept them steady.

He stared into her lavender eyes, wondering what they saw, how they'd looked before, then wanted to kick himself. It didn't matter what color her eyes were; purple, blue, or polka dot. She was their female. Theirs for the rest of their lives and beyond. No other had been created for them. "Sky, you can tell us anything and know there will be no judging, no doubting, nothing but what you should've always had from those who were supposed to love and cherish you. I know you didn't have that growing up, but from this point on, you'll never have to doubt either of our words."

Her mouth opened, but before she could pull her lip between her teeth, he was there, taking that little bit of flesh into his own mouth, licking, nibbling, and sucking before releasing. "If anyone is going to be biting you, it's going to be me or my brother," he growled, wanting to do more than just bite her lip. Fuck, her scent spiked, the sweet smell of female arousal soaking into his senses.

"You both turn me inside out without even trying. I don't...I'm not...it's just that. I want to know you better. Does that make sense?"

He wanted to howl and say they already knew each other. Her wolf knew theirs. It was instinctual. The rest would work itself out in time, but patience would win them her heart. Oh, there was no doubt she felt something for them, but he didn't want her to accept them because of their animals. They wanted the woman as well. Fuck, his hand was going to be getting a work out. He met Raydon's gaze, understanding flowing between them without words.

"Hellmouth, you can have anything you need, except other males." Raydon's tone was hard, uncompromising. Neither of them could give her that. Hell, no shifter could stand by and allow their mate to be with another without a killing rage taking over.

Sky rolled her eyes, her hands going to hips too narrow for his liking. "First of all, boys, if I had wanted other males, I sure as shit wouldn't have been tracking you both." She stopped, her right hand flying to her mouth as red tinted her cheeks. "I so did not just say that out loud. Pretend you didn't hear that."

Raydon moved in next to Sky, his hand moving hers off her mouth. "Oh no, there's no takebacks. How about you expand on that little announcement?"

Sky shook her head back and forth, her lips rolling into her mouth in a comical way, those purple eyes of hers glittering with laughter.

"Even if you don't say anything else, we both now have hope. Do you know what hope does for a wolf, baby?" River asked, tracing her cheek down her jaw not waiting for her to answer. "Hope makes us even more possessive, makes us want to stamp our presence all over you so there's not a question of who you belong to."

Her brow rose. "That goes both, or should I say three ways." Her little wolf-like growl was music to both he and his brother's ears.

"As it should. Since we caught your scent running all those months ago, you're the only female we've wanted." Raydon's finger traced her cheek like he'd done, only he lifted her chin, bringing her face toward him. "We can give you time, but space isn't an option. Where you go, one of us will be with you. Is that going to be a problem?"

Her chest rose and fell. Seconds ticked by while she thought. River was sure she was going to balk, but then she nodded. "I agree, but you can't try to be my dad. I don't want or need a daddy."

Raydon grinned. The look so damn wicked he wondered if Sky even realized what she'd done. "Hellmouth, I have never had any intention to play daddy to your little girl. Now, if you want to do some role playing, I'm game for anything." He spread his arms wide, his smile letting her know he wasn't joking.

Sky's head looked at Raydon then him. No way in hell was he saying a damn word. Not with the way his cock was hard as a pole in his jeans. The image of the three of them rolling around on their custom bed, playing out each and every fantasy they'd ever had, was enough to make him ready to come in his jeans like a prepubescent teen.

"What's the plan for today?" he asked, trying to get his mind on something else while adjusting his dick when her eyes went down then back up. "Try to ignore him. You mentioned role playing and images of you naked had Mr. B ready to roll."

"Mr. B?" she asked.

River shrugged. "I didn't want to name him Mr. Big and have people thinking I had an overinflated ego to go with my overinflated dick. So, Mr. B it was."

Raydon snorted. "Seriously, how the hell did you block that from me?"

"Easy, you didn't block yours, which was a stupid name, so giving you shit over it kept you distracted." River pulled Sky in front of him, waiting for the inevitable question to come. Their little mate didn't disappoint.

"What's his name?" She pointed toward Raydon's dick, the visible bulge as clear as River's.

His brother growled, but there was no heat behind the sound. "Vlad," he grunted.

Silence fell between them. River didn't so much as breathe, waiting to see what Sky did or said before he put his two cents in.

She didn't disappoint, her laughter rang through the room, filling every empty space. "Oh my gawd. Like the Impaler? I love it." She launched herself into his arms.

Raydon's eyes widened, then he was lifting Sky into his arms, pulling her legs around his waist, taking advantage of her position in only a way a crafty male could. River grinned, shaking his head. "Seriously, you get jumped on for that, while my name got scoffed at? Harsh, man." He ran his hand down Sky's back, making sure she knew he was playing while he left her and Raydon alone. He'd known since they were kids they'd share a mate, or at least suspected. They'd shared everything since conception. Sure, they didn't always share a female, but when they didn't, he'd felt as if something was missing. That something had not only been the wrong female, but also the twin connection. Being able to take care of a female completely with the love and trust of another, that was connected to you on a visceral level, made things deeper, in his opinion.

"My turn," River muttered, his hands moved over Sky, taking her from Raydon like they'd done it a thousand times. Raydon didn't protest, knowing he'd get his time as well.

Raydon smoothed his hand over Sky's ass before he walked out of the room, his mind staying connected to the two people who meant more to him than any other.

River kissed Sky, aware his twin was watching. Hell, he kissed her for the both of them. If Raydon wanted to feel what he was, all he had to do was connect with him, and he'd be there. However, as he walked with their little female wrapped around him, he didn't feel his brother tapping into their link. Sky's moan brought his attention back to her. With each step he took, his dick jerked, demanding to be let out. River hated to deny the appendage anything, but he wouldn't be getting any attention anytime soon. They wanted to ease Sky into their relationship even though most wolves didn't, letting their instincts guide them. With all the things she'd been through, he and Raydon wanted to make sure she was one hundred percent onboard. From the way she kissed him back and ground her sweet little body against him, there wasn't a single doubt her body was ready. Pulling back took a lot more control than he'd had to exert in a long time, especially when she whimpered and chased his lips with her own. "Easy, we have all the time in the world to explore each other. For now, let's feed another appetite."

His wolf howled, raking at his insides and calling him all kinds of a fool as he looked down into sparkling purple eyes. Fuck, he almost said screw being a gentleman and tossed Sky over his shoulder. In their bedroom, he'd feast on her with his lips, and body, then call his brother in to bring them food. Maybe he'd be satisfied enough he'd be able to roll over and give his brother room.

"Keep thinking that way, and I'll beat your ass," Raydon rumbled through their link. *"Besides, she's starving."*

"You two are doing that twin thing, aren't you?" Sky tugged on his ear.

"Hey, it's not me, it's him." River shifted her in his arms, loving the feel of her in his embrace.

She rolled her eyes, a grin splitting her lips. "I bet when you two were growing up, you played that card all the time."

River froze for a split second, shuttered his eyes and his memories. "We only had each other for a long time. I guess it's like second nature to speak to each other through our link. We will work on including you though. As our mate, we shouldn't be rude like that."

He turned from the wall he had Sky pressed against and made the way into the kitchen where he could smell the scent of bacon and eggs.

Gourmet cooks weren't on the list of things either man had wanted to be, but they could get by. Raydon already had a plate piled with bacon and a pan with scrambled eggs half done. They each liked scrambled eggs with cheese on top. Shit, they hadn't asked Sky her preference.

Raydon pointed the spatula he held at them. "How do you like your eggs, hellmouth? I can make scrambled like a rockstar, over easy not too bad, but get fancy and you're fucked, and not in a good way." He winked.

Sky laughed. "I like scrambled with cheese and some picante sauce on the side."

Raydon held the spatula against his chest and folded his hands as if he was in prayer. "Thank you, Goddess, for giving me a beautiful mate, but also a mate who is smart and doesn't fuck with eggs."

"Did you think I'd ask for something like, eggs benedict or what?" She wiggled on the counter where River sat her, joy emanating from her eyes.

His brother shrugged. "I'd have tried to make them if that's what you wanted, but I wouldn't have promised they'd have been good."

Sky lifted her bare foot, hooking it around Raydon, uncaring about popping grease. "The fact you'd have made it for me, would've made it taste great."

River coughed into his hand, the word bullshit smothered by his coughing.

"Hey, you calling me a liar, sir?" She raised her foot she'd had hooked around Raydon, the tips of her toenails had been painted, by one of the other ladies, a shocking orange. He wasn't sure if Sky had even noticed until her eyes widened. "Who the hell did that, and why the fuck did they paint them orange?" She shuddered comically.

His brother snorted, flipped the huge pan of eggs over at once but didn't answer.

"Ah, hellmouth, Joni said you needed a little color on your pale ass, her words not mine. But the only color that was on hand was orange since Halloween was the last holiday any of the ladies had celebrated, or some shit. I told them to leave your feet alone, but again, we were overruled. When one of your friends said you wouldn't appreciate us if you woke up to gnarly feet, we just nodded and let them do as they wanted, barring you weren't harmed." He couldn't keep the growl from his tone at the end.

"I can so hear Joni and Taryn saying that, those bitches," she said with affection.

The toaster popped with four slices of bread, a perfect gold, next to Sky. She didn't need to be asked, just started buttering them and placing them on the plate with the others. It was all so normal, so domestic, he had to turn away. "What would you like to drink?" he asked, turning from the vision of her was hard.

"Coffee with a side of coffee, a splash of milk and some sugar." She laughed.

He looked back to see her legs swinging back and forth, no sign of discomfort. His brother looked toward him, a brow raised in question. He turned away, grabbing three cups out of the cabinet, pouring them each a cup of coffee, giving her a splash of milk. "Here you go." He handed one cup to Raydon, then took his and Sky's to the center island. "Sugar is right here." The little dish they kept on the counter held three different variety of sweetners. He made note of which one she took, mentally checking their stock.

"Alright, let's eat. You gonna sit up there and chow or want to eat at the table?" Raydon asked, pointing toward the big wooden table set up off to the side of the kitchen.

"Do you guys eat there often?" Sky snagged a piece of bacon, chewing delicately while Raydon transferred food onto plates.

"Nah, we usually only eat there when guests come over or when we want to impress someone, which has been...never, until now. We tend to eat at the bar here." River tipped his chin toward the barstools.

Sky swallowed the bite in her mouth. "I like that better. Seems more intimate. Besides at that big table, where would I sit if you both sat at the heads? I'd be like the monkey in the middle." Her face turned pink then red as her words hit them all.

"Hellmouth, you would never be the monkey in the middle. Female, our mate, but never monkey," Raydon growled, pulling her toward him, the food forgotten.

River made sure his twin had turned all the burners off then proceeded to get the plates and silverware set up. Through their link, he felt his twin's satisfaction as Sky accepted his domination. She may be a badass part dragon, wolf, human, but she gave to them what they needed. They wouldn't take her or her gifts for granted.

He dished a helping of cheesy eggs onto Sky's plate along with bacon and toast, then did his own, sitting down with his cup of coffee and waited for his brother to finish making out with Sky. When it seemed Rye wasn't in any hurry, but he could feel Sky's hunger, he growled. "Our female is hungry and needs food, brother."

Raydon grunted, but after another minute, he and Sky came around the counter, then they all three dug into the meal, moaning in unison as they filled their bellies with perfectly seasoned eggs and bacon, cooked just right.

Sky pushed her plate away. "What's on the agenda for today? And no, I'm not ready for that." Her eyes glowed, saying she wasn't really sure, but River didn't push.

"You asked that before, but we got distracted," Raydon laughed.

She giggled, remembering why they'd gotten distracted. Their names for their dicks. "I hope you both realize I'll be using that knowledge at some point in the future. Unless you want others to know, you best give me what I want, when I want, and no, that doesn't mean in the bedroom. However, I will reserve that as well."

River pushed his plate away, then tugged her into his arms. "Hellmouth, you've got some things to learn about us. First thing, we don't need a bed or our bedroom to want to make love to you. Second thing, we don't embarrass easily, and third," he paused for a moment. "We always get even."

There was no doubt what he was talking about as he spoke and shifted her on his thick thighs, letting her feel what she could only describe as a third leg. Holy shitnshynoma, no way in hell could she take that, and surely, its twin at the same time.

"Hey, what's wrong?" River gripped her chin between his thumb and finger.

How was she supposed tell him this mating wasn't going to happen, when not only their wolves wanted it, but so did she and that bit of dragon inside her. She bit her lip, shaking her head.

"You can tell us anything, love," he spoke softly like he was talking to an injured animal.

Raydon reached over, pulling her lip from between her teeth. "Hellmouth, tell us what's made your scent so damn offensive. Whatever it is, we will fix it."

She hated this fear, the uncertainty, the feeling she'd felt since she'd been a little girl under Keith's wrath. Goddess, she was tired of being less than, of being the wimpy wolf. "What if I can't be what you need?" That was as close to what she felt that she'd say out loud.

River looked at Raydon, but she didn't sense them speaking to each other, which was good.

"The Goddess wouldn't have created you for us if you weren't meant for us. If she didn't think you weren't the piece we were missing, then she wouldn't have sent you here. Our entire life, we've known there was a piece of us that was out there. When we scented you, even if our alpha had forbidden it, we'd have hunted you to the ends of the

Earth, or beyond, to find you. You're that perfect one. The female who soothes the ragged edges we both have, making us level."

"That's a lot to put on me." She looked from one man to the other, sincerity shown in their gorgeous eyes. Goddess, she truly was a fool if she didn't give them a chance. Hell, what was she saying? She was doing more than giving them a try, she was going to give them her all and prayed she didn't screw things up.

"That's better," River said.

Before she could ask what he was talking about, he lifted her until she was straddling his lap, making her acutely aware the only thing separating her flesh from his extremely large dick was his jeans and possibly his underwear. Did they wear underwear, or were they commando men? The question had her leaning backward. "If you kiss me like you mean it, I'm afraid you'll have me over this counter in no time flat. I want to...get to know you both, first. Does that sound stupid?"

Raydon chuckled, the deep sound eased some of her fears. "Hellmouth, the fact you didn't tell him to fuck off was a good start. How about you get dressed and we head into town for a little pseudo date, while River and I clean up in here?"

She grasped onto the reprieve with both hands, then reality struck. "I don't have any clothes."

River spun on the stool with her in his arms, setting her feet on the cool tile. "Actually, you do. While you were out of it, Taryn brought a few of your things here."

She saw a little color bloom on his cheeks at the admission and fell a little more in love with him, but she wasn't going to let him off the hook that easily. "Then why didn't you give me something of mine to sleep in?"

His smile turned positively wolfish. "Because I wanted my scent on you while you slept."

And just like that, she turned to a pile of goo. Gah, one of these gorgeous men was bad enough, but two? She had no chance of saying no to anything they wanted. Of course, she didn't think she would ever want to. A small voice inside her head gave a mocking laugh, the sound familiar but grating. Sky frowned, lifting her hand to her temple as she stepped away from River.

"You alright, love?" Raydon asked, his hands settled on her hips, stopping her backward motion.

She nodded, then shook her head, then nodded. "Yeah, I'm fine. I'm going to take a quick shower and get dressed. Where are my clothes again?"

River and Raydon glanced at one another, then back at her, making her angry. "Don't do that twin talk."

Raydon's hands tightened on her while River lifted his arms up. River spoke first. "We said we wouldn't, and we won't." The words, *unless it was for her safety,* was left unsaid.

An argument was the last thing she wanted, yet for some unknown reason a little part of her longed to...incite one, which was so unlike her. A slight pain stabbed her behind her right eye, but she didn't let the guys know, hiding the discomfort behind a smile. "Sorry, I'll feel better once I'm showered and dressed in my own things."

Leaning up on her toes, she pulled first River down for a swift kiss, then did the same with Raydon. She could feel the heat of their gazes while she hurried away. The pain eased the further away from them she got, but the voice inside her head reminded her of the nightmare. Without thinking about it, she began building a wall between her conscious mind and the other female she could feel waiting to pounce, in her mind. She didn't know why, but she felt an urgent need to keep it blocked. Once she was sure the wall was thick and impenetrable, she grabbed her things out of the places her guys had said they'd be. "I should probably be mad, but I'm not," she whispered, smiling at the neat rows of her things hanging across from theirs. Her guys were organizers. She ran her hand over their shirts, all color coordinated from black, to navy, to grey and then a few other colors. She wondered if they had their names inside, so they didn't wear each other's, then dismissed the questions.

"Shower, then questions." Why she was talking to herself she didn't know, but for whatever reason, she didn't want to be inside her own head.

Once her shower was done, she grabbed a fluffy towel off a heated rack. The fact they had one was amazing and showed how different their lives were. Yes, her family had money, but they weren't allowed to have such things, not under Keith's rule. He was a bastard of the first order. "Gah, I'm so glad he's dead." Her wolf snarled in agreement.

At the mirror, she wiped the fog off so she could see herself in the light of day, without the need to hurry. Her mind whirled as she saw a red tint on the right half of her torso, even on the back half. Luckily her face didn't have the weird rash, if you could call it that as the weird mark literally covered her right side, bisecting her with a straight line down the middle, not like a rash would with some bleeding onto one side or the other. She ran her hand over the redness, worrying there'd be raised skin, but there was nothing but smooth flesh beneath her fingers. Worry had her reaching for Lula through their link. "*Lula, I need you.*" If this was part of her dragon manifesting itself, surely the dragon female would know.

Seconds turned to minutes with no response from Lula. Panic had her breath whooshing in and out of her lungs. "Easy, she's probably off doing dragon things. This is probably normal." She tried to reassure herself, but that other voice in her head seemed to laugh at her. Sky sent a bolt of fire over the wall, making the other screech and retreat.

Her right side heated up but didn't appear injured. "Alright, just wait for Lula to contact you. All's fine." She gave a nod at her odd reflection, then picked the towel back up. Fuck, what would her guys think when they saw her body? "Cross that bridge when you get there, and stop talking to yourself," she admonished herself.

She left the bathroom, got dressed without looking at herself again. No need to look when she knew her two toned image was still there. Luckily, her face was unmarred. Hell, she'd have to invest in some really good makeup in order to cover that up. Sephora would be her new best friend. She laughed, getting her head stuck while she tried to pull the sweater over her head. "Oh for fuckssake."

"Need a little help, hellmouth?" River's hands pulled the sweater over her head, the slouchy thing finally settled over her properly.

"Thank you. I thought I was going to suffocate." Hell, she was actually glad she'd put a tank on under the sweater, first, otherwise there was no way he'd not have noticed the red half of her torso. She wasn't ready to answer questions yet.

Chapter Five

Sky walked out of the bedroom holding River's hand. The calluses rubbed against her softer ones, making her wonder what they'd feel like on her other parts.

"Hmm, whatcha thinking about?" he asked.

She shivered at the deep timbre in his tone. "I'm so not answering that question, and since you and I both know our sense of smell is great, you must know I was thinking of...well, anyway. Let's move along, shall we?" She swung their hands in a wide arc, laughing as he grumbled beneath his breath about injuring Mr. B. Today, they'd have a normal day if it was the last thing she did. Well, normal as a female dating two gorgeous twins.

"There you two are. Damn, you look gorgeous, hellmouth," Raydon murmured, stepping in front of her. His hands cradled her face. "You smell even better, and I don't mean like freshly showered either." His nostrils flared, letting her know he could scent her need.

Sky slapped at his chest. "A gentleman doesn't mention such things."

Raydon bent, placing his lips next to her ear. "Never professed to be a gentleman, love." He bit the lobe, then traced it with his tongue. "Let's go before I forget my promise."

She tilted her head to the side. "What promise?"

River laughed. "We promised to take it slow and let you lead. However, if you keep smelling like need and want, he and I will both need to visit the bathroom for a cold shower and a hand to dick visit with ourselves even though we really want you."

She snorted, then laughed as the two men growled.

"A hand to dick visit? I've never heard of that described in such a way." She wiped tears of mirth from beneath her eyes.

Raydon punched River in the arm. "Brother, we don't tell our female we're gonna jackoff."

Sky grabbed River's hand before he could hit Raydon back. "You promised me a date. Besides, I know all about men and their need to wash their err, privates, really fast." She let go of River, moving quickly toward the door to the garage before they could grab her. "You coming?"

Both men grumbled something that sounded suspiciously like not yet, but she ignored it, enjoying the ability to tease them without fear.

"What are we driving?" Sky asked.

River held a set of keys in his hand. "My Raptor."

She looked from one to the other, not knowing what the heck that was. "A bird?" Sure, she had some dragon in her, but like Lula, she didn't think it took keys.

Raydon slapped River on the back. "She's not a woman impressed with vehicles, bro."

Shaking his head, River grabbed her hand before leading the way out the door. Inside their garage sat two Harley's, Raydon's Monster Truck, Sky's little car, and his Ford Raptor.

Raydon moved ahead of them. "That's his baby that he's spent way too much on buying then customizing."

River flipped Raydon off, pushing past him with a smirk. "Come on, hellmouth, I'll show you my girl. See that matte black beauty?" He pointed out his rig. At her nod, he continued. "That's Ebony. She's your chariot, built to my specifications. She can pretty much handle just about anything."

Sky touched her temple, then his, asking without words to see what he meant. Once he opened his mind, she could see all he spoke of. The steel frame he'd had tweaked, the bulletproof windows, and so much more her mind whirled with it all. She didn't understand what all she saw, but was aware he'd had basically everything modified to where his truck was nothing like one off the assembly line. She was almost afraid to touch it.

"Baby, what's ours is yours," River whispered, lifting her face with a finger beneath her chin. "Never fear touching anything, and I mean anything you want." He winked, then lifted her into the drivers' side. "Scoot to the middle unless you want to drive?"

Her face felt hot at all the things she would be touching someday soon, then she pictured herself trying to navigate the huge truck, which had her shifting over. Both men climbed in beside her, each so much alike, yet different. "Thank you for...everything," she said, once they were on the road to town.

Raydon rested one hand on her thigh, while River held her hand in his over his hard leg. The other he kept on the wheel as he drove, the confidence bespoke of experience. Neither man responded for a few seconds. The air seemed to swirl with emotions she couldn't translate quickly enough.

River lifted their joined hands. "Sky, we've waited what seemed a lifetime for you, although we're younger than some who're still looking. What makes it different for Rye and me is," he sighed before continuing. "We didn't think we'd find a female who was perfect like you. We don't mean in looks, but never doubt we think you're the most beautiful woman in all the universes. What I, we, mean is that, we'd always had a connection that most didn't understand, a connection that was more than just a twin thing. More than a shifter connection. He didn't have to reach out to me for me to hear him or vice versa. We knew instinctively when one needed the other, sometimes before we knew ourselves. That probably doesn't even make sense," he growled.

Raydon gave a dry chuckle. "You're doing fine, bro. Sky, we'd almost resolved that our lives would be split in half with separate mates, even though our wolves snarled at the thought. Then one night, on a dark and cloudy evening, we both scented the most alluring female, and we both knew without a doubt our world would forever be linked by one female. That was you, Sky." His lips brushed her knuckles. "We can wait until you're ready as long as you're near and safe."

She blinked back stupid tears. She didn't deserve one, let alone two such amazing men. However, she'd be damned if she didn't grab hold of what they were offering and hold on with both hands, or paws, whatever she had to in order to keep them. "I'm so lucky," she whispered.

Raydon's fingers itched to shift and do some damage, hating the fact Sky like all the other members of Keith's fucked up pack thought they were unworthy. If the fucker hadn't been dead already, he'd find a way to kill him. Hell, he wanted to dig up his ashes and spit on them for good measure, but the Fey of the Mystic Pack had done some magic shit to the bastard's remains, saying they wanted to insure he had no way of coming back. He was all for the fucker never coming back, but damned if he didn't want to fuck him up all over again.

The feel of his mate's eyes on him had him releasing the strangle hold he had on the door handle one finger at a time. "So, what's the plan once we get where we're going?"

River looked at him then Sky. "I'm game for whatever she is so long as it's safe."

Rye nodded, trying to get his shit together before meeting her purple gaze. "What would you like to do?" Most females liked to shop, but he didn't think Sky would. Besides, Sturgis didn't have a large mall per se, but they'd both agreed they'd do what they could to accommodate her wishes.

"Let's see how things feel when we get there." Trepidation laced her tone.

His fingers traced the inner edge of her thigh, making her shiver. "There's no need to worry, hellmouth. Between the three of us, nothing and no one will fuck with you or us," he growled. Hell, he dared anyone say a word that would make Sky the slightest bit uncomfortable. Either he or River would be more than happy to teach them the error of their ways with their fist or claws.

"Easy tiger." She patted his chest.

Raydon released his hold on her thigh, capturing her small hand to his chest. "Wolf, baby." He snapped his teeth together. "We're wolves."

Her laughter filled the cab. "Why do all of you have such issues with cats?"

River mocked sneezed. "I'm allergic to them."

"What if I had a love of all things feline and was a crazy cat lady who had like, ten of them back at my house?" She looked over her shoulder at River.

Raydon looked down at Sky, then at his twin. "We'd find a nice cat sanctuary for them and give a huge amount of money so they'd take care of them for you," he said with a grin.

"You um, don't though, do you?" River asked with a frown.

Sky shook her head. "You guys are too easy. The only pets I was ever allowed were imaginary, and no, they most certainly were not cats. I always wanted a monkey though."

This time it was Raydon who shivered. "Woman, have you been to the zoo? Monkeys throw their shit at you. Hell, at the San Diego zoo we saw monkeys sticking their fingers in...needless to say, it scarred me for life. No monkeys for me. Nope." He shuddered again as he remembered the monkeys in question and what they did after they'd...he almost gagged, refraining, barely.

"Oh my gawd, they did not eat their own shit?" Sky asked, eyes wide.

Raydon realized he'd allowed the memory to flow through their trio link. His twin was glaring at him.

"Thanks a lot, bro, I'd had that memory buried so deep I'd forgotten it until just now. Gonna need to see a therapist." River made a gagging sound, which had Sky giggling.

Although it really had been one of the nastiest things he'd seen, especially as a six year old impressionable kid, he'd replay it again, if for nothing else but to see their mate's eyes shine with happiness.

"Hey, speak, or think for yourself. Warn me next time, so I can block your ass," River grumbled, but he too was smiling.

"You two are nuts, but you're my nuts," Sky joked, then her hand covered her mouth. "Oh lord, don't even say it."

Raydon raised one brow in question, realization hitting both he and River at the same time. She'd not only called them her nuts, but she'd made a sexual reference, sort of. "Baby, we'd never do any such thing as say something so immature as deez nuts. Right River?"

River made a zipping motion with his fingers to his lips. "Nope, never."

River slowed down as they reached the city limits. They both scanned the area for any signs of threats. Winter was still in full force, but with Christmas over, most of the tourists had headed home. Although the Mystic Lodge continued to fill up with people wanting to ski and get away for long weekends, and more frequently businesses booking for company retreats, Sturgis wasn't packed the way it was in the summer. His brother parked along the business side, knowing they'd be able to walk along the sidewalks and do some window shopping without having to cross the busy road. Although they'd brought most of her things from her home, they'd agreed she needed some essentials.

"We can stop and grab anything you need. If you can't find it, we'll make a list of whatever it is then order online. Or, if you want to, we can go a little further outside of town and find a big mall."

Their mate's scent went from happy to sad in seconds. "I don't need anything, thanks."

River stepped in front of her, placing his back to anyone coming toward them. "Sky, we know what you have and don't have. Remember, we had weeks to watch over you and obsess over every little detail. We also know what that bastard of a pretend alpha did to all of you. As our mate, it's our duty to provide for you. Now, before you get your fur in an uproar, or wings...goddess, I really would love to see that—don't get mad," he implored before continuing. "We're thirty years old. We've literally worked since we were twelve years old, saving every penny we had. That beast of a truck we rode down in? That's been my one and only big splurge. Rye's huge rig is a pile of junk compared to Ebony, but it's no junker. We buy very little, except things that mean a lot to us. So, our bikes and trucks are about it. Our home? We would sell it in a minute if you didn't like it. For eighteen years, give or take, we've worked, and we've saved so we could provide for our mate. That's not to say our female can't and won't be allowed to work. And no, I'm not saying we'll be your lords and masters by saying *allowed*. Fuck, Rye, help a brother out here."

Raydon wiped the smile from his lips. "I think you get the gist of what he's saying, what we mean. The one and only thing that means the most to us, is you. Not some nameless faceless female anymore, but you, Sky. If you want to go to school, we support you in that decision. You want to start your own internet business selling baby bows, tell us what you need, and we'll get it. Or, if you want to be a lady of leisure, we're fine with that. Whatever you decide you want to do, we will support you. As long as you're safe and happy, then we'll be happy. Well, as long as you're with us I should add."

"How about we just stroll the sidewalks and pretend like we're normal for a while?" Her voice shook, but she stood straight like the alpha female that resided inside her.

The longing in her tone had him wanting to give her anything. "We can do that. Are you cold?" he asked, their breaths making clouds when they spoke.

Sky tossed her head back and laughed, then stood on her toes while she tugged him down with a firm grip on the front of his flannel shirt. "Aw, is the wolfman cold? Newsflash, I've got dragon blood running through my veins. I don't think I'll ever be cold again. Seriously, I had to learn to regulate my body all over again when I was with the Fey. Luckily Lula was a very patient teacher. I think she only called me little wolagon a couple times. Goddess, she's seriously a little demented, but a hundred percent amazing."

"Wolagon?" River asked from beside them.

Sky looked over at him. "She was trying out all kinds of combination names like Jenna's Wolpires. I told her wolagon was a no go for me. She said she was still working on it."

River bit his lip. "I don't know, I kinda like it. Our little wolagon is pretty cute." He ruffled her hair.

Raydon lifted her up with his hands on her hips, bringing her face in line with his. "How about Wolfagon? I agree that wolagon sounds too much like hooligan, so that's definitely a no for me."

She licked her lips, their breaths mingling in the cold air. "I like it," she agreed.

Without thinking, he sealed their lips together right there in the middle of town, uncaring who was watching.

"Alright you two, unless you want to draw a crowd, let's roll, and try to act like we're normal instead of two horny twins with poles in our jeans, sandwiching the most gorgeous female between us." River clapped his hands together, rubbing them back and forth as if he were cold while he spoke.

"Afternoon, Mr. Thompson. Lovely day for a stroll, yeah?"

Raydon heard his brother's words, hating to separate from the heaven that was Sky's lips, but knew River was right. Hell, if he continued exploring the sweet taste of their mate, he'd want to taste more, and that could lead to trouble. "Come on, hellmouth, although I might have to change your nickname to sweetmouth. Damn, you taste divine."

"You're such a sweet talker." She pressed her lips to his one more time before wiggling to be free. "I wonder what movies are playing?"

River and Raydon both groaned.

"Don't tell me you don't like going to the movies. Imagine, sitting in a dark theater, me between you two, watching a sexy movie, getting all excited. I casually take one of each of your hands and place them on my thighs. Did I mention I would be really excited to be watching a movie with two sexy men?" She skipped forward, turning to walk backward to watch them as she spoke.

"Question? Are there other people in the theater with us?" River asked.

Sky shrugged, her purple eyes shining. "Maybe, but to me there'd only be the three of us."

Right then and there, Raydon knew he was hopelessly in love with their mate, and he knew they'd be taking her to the movies or anywhere she wanted.

Their bond flared between the three of them, giving River hope that it was more than just that, a bond. Love, goddess, love flowed from his twin toward Sky. River had felt the first stirrings for Sky when they'd scented her. It was how he and his wolf worked. Love and mating was one and the same to him. His heart had searched for hers and found her to be the one. Raydon was the thinker, the one who held back. River had no doubt things would fall into place. He hoped sooner rather than later, but damn, even he was shocked at the sudden flow of emotion.

"What's that?" Sky asked abruptly, her hand covering her heart.

River went to her first. "That's our bond, strengthening."

Her gaze darted from him to Raydon, who wore a frown. "I didn't expect...what I mean is. Shit, I'm gonna fuck up this time," Raydon tried to explain.

Sky held her hand out to him. "We're all new to this. Heck, I think everyone is new to our situation. Let's not compare what we have to anyone else, okay? We just go with what feels right and communicate, nothing held back." Her eyes darted away from them toward the road.

Pulling her into his body, he held her close, hugging her while his eyes met Raydon's. They honored her wishes, keeping their twin link closed. However, his brother caught the emotion flaring from Sky when she'd spoken. Was she hiding something from them? Raydon shook his head, keeping River from searching for answers. It was their first outing as a trio and neither of them wanted to ruin their time. If she had a secret, time would reveal it. Mates couldn't hide things from one another, not true mates like they were. Once they mated with her fully, they'd know all there was to know about her and vice versa. River couldn't wait, yet he wanted to make sure she was ready. Time was something they had in abundance now that they'd found her and eliminated the threat against her and her old pack. Hell, she was part motherfucking dragon. She could probably slay all of them if pissed. The thought should've been sobering.

"Want to check out the theater for movies and showtimes?" Raydon asked, stepping next to Sky, taking her hand in his. No matter how odd they might look, River took her other hand. They were a trio and would be damned if they hid it from the world.

"I'd love that." Sky swung their joined hands back and forth while they walked.

River kept his focus on their surroundings while they talked and listened to Sky exclaim over Raydon's stories of their childhood. "Asshole, I didn't scream like a girl when that happened. That was you. Sky, he's the one who screamed like a little bitch when a bear jumped out of the woods at us. We were on vacation up in Wyoming with our parents and some others when he." River paused, pointing at his twin. "Raydon, the asswipe, decided it would be a good idea to check out a cave. I told him I thought it smelled funny, but noooo, did he listen to me?

All of a sudden, a roar that shook the damn ground sounded, and a furry wolf came flying by me. I'd read somewhere that the safest thing to do was take the fetal position. Again, I said fuck that, fuck that, fuck that, which I got my mouth washed out for later. I then shifted faster than I'd ever done, shredding my clothes and passed Raydon like he was in slowmo. In my head, all I heard was him crying like a bitch for me to wait up." Through their link, he showed her his memories, letting her see and feel what he'd felt at the time, tempering his fear so she wouldn't be afraid.

"Hey, this was my story, jackass. Why'd you go and ruin it?" Raydon smacked River on the back of the head.

River did the same, making his brother grunt. They'd always play fought, never really hurting the other.

As Raydon grunted, River opened his mouth to tease, only to find himself pressed against an invisible shield a couple feet away, while Raydon was shoved against the wall of the building, looking as stunned as he. Neither of them could move. Their mate stood with her arms out from her sides, her head whipped back and forth glaring at them. "You do not hurt each other, ever." Her voice sounded deeper than Sky's, angry.

When he opened his mouth, nothing came out. The same thing appeared to affect Raydon. Through their link, he tried connecting to Sky, but came to a hard stop at a wall. *"Rye, can you connect with Sky?"* he asked through their twin link.

Raydon shook his head, the muscles in his arms bulging as he tried to free himself from her hold. Finally, her name came out in a whisper, making Sky turn toward his brother, giving River a chance to break free from her hold.

"Sky, we'd never hurt each other or you. We were just playing; brothers do that sort of thing. Look into my mind or Raydon's. You can see we love each other and would never cause harm to one another."

River stepped closer, hoping to get through to her without her lashing out at him.

Their mate shook her head, then seemed to deflate; there was no other word for what happened to her. "What's going on?" Sky asked, her head whipping back and forth between them.

Raydon stepped away from the wall, shaking his arms out like a fighter would. "What do you remember, love?"

She looked at the ground then River. "I...we were walking and you two were joking around, then darkness. Am I going crazy?"

River pulled her into his arms. "No, baby, you've just got to adjust to a lot of new shit. We need to be more conscientious."

A growl that would make any wolf proud came out of Sky. "I don't want everyone to think they have to wear kid gloves with me or walk on egg shells. Dammit, I'm not a freaking weakling." The word *anymore* floated into their connection, but none of them acknowledged it.

"Alright, this is what we're gonna do. We're going to go to Chaps, get a drink, and find out what movies are playing. Then, we're going to go to whatever we can all agree on, 'cause this isn't a sheocracy, even though we want to get into your pants. Then, if you're really good, we'll make you come while watching the show."

Sky laughed, then covered her mouth when she snorted loudly. "A sheocracy?" she questioned.

River nodded, taking her hand. "Yep, it's she and democracy put together. Women have magical pussies. Therefore, we men have to do as they say or hand to dick time. Hence, sheocracy. My hand and dick have been dating a long ass time. I will not be bullied into a sheocracy." He winked. "Unless of course you wanted to sit on my lap during the movie, nekkid," he joked.

Between her laughter and Raydon's groan, they made it to Chaps with only a few verbal jabs at him for his words. "Looks like we weren't the only ones with the idea to come in for a drink." River looked at the line of vehicles outside the bar and then at Raydon.

"You good, hellmouth? We can go somewhere else." He looked down the block, seeing the other bars had a few cars and trucks in front of them, but nothing like Chaps.

"I'm good, guys, really. Let's get a drink and find out showtimes. I wonder if there's like a matinee of The Notebook or something like that?"

Raydon growled as he opened the door. "Not happening, cupcake. Magical pussy or no, I'm not watching that movie in a theater. At home with a bowl of popcorn, a naked you, me, and River, maybe, but not to-day, cupcake, not today."

Chapter Six

River scanned the inside of the bar, wondering why half of the Mystic Wolves pack were there. Hell, there were probably more like three quarters, but who was counting? They made their way to the bar, finding two stools open. Raydon took a seat, pulling Sky onto his lap with a murmured explanation about space and River being too big to sit on his lap.

"What's going on? Why's everyone here, and why weren't we invited to the party?" he asked Jett Tremaine.

Jett sat three bottles of beer in front of them before answering. "The ladies decided they needed a girls' day out, which means the guys had to come into town as well. You know, because ain't none of them fuckers able to stay at home when their women are gone. Then Taryn was challenged by a couple chicks to a dance off. I mean, what the fuck, right? So, they had their dance off, Taryn won, of course. The other chicks got pissed, demanded a redo. It was a shitshow, to which Talia had to come and intervene. Goddess, I love that mama Fey. Anyway, now the women are all drunk and sleeping it off in the backroom. Oh, did I mention the Fey can add some sparkle shit to drinks that get shifters shitfaced? Yep, it can, and it did. So, now I got a bar full of asshole men." He gave Bronx a two-finger wave, then flipped him the bird. "Who ain't gonna be getting laid tonight. Bottoms up, kids, there ain't no Fey dust in these drinks." Jett finished with a slam of his hands on the bar top, a wicked glint in his eyes.

"Well...shit, I'm glad we weren't invited." River turned on the stool, observing the room at large. Grouped around the pool tables were several male shifters, playing pool and drinking. The dance floor was empty save for a few human women. "Do you know what's playing at the theater in town?"

Torq stomped by, coughing into his hand what sounded like pussy-whipped but didn't stop to talk.

"Where's he going?" Sky asked.

"Probably to check on his mate. She's in the back with the others having drank a lot of the fey laced beer. I contacted Niall and Zayn once they were all passed out, but both men told me to handle it. I'm handling it like a boss, yep." He gave another two-finger wave when someone yelled out they needed a refill, this time with both hands that ended with his middle fingers up. "All these motherfuckers here are so damn needy. Come get your own damn drinks, I ain't your waitress, ass-munch."

"Err, I think you're supposed to be serving them, not calling them names?" Sky offered.

Jett leaned on the bar with his arms crossed. "You want to become a waitress for the evening?" He jerked his head up as another guy yelled out his drink order.

River and Raydon downed their beer, slamming their empty bottles on the counter. "Nope, not our female."

Sky grabbed her own bottle, drinking a huge swallow, taking a breath before speaking. "I'm gonna have to decline." She chugged the rest of her drink, slamming the empty down like the twins, then burped loudly. "Oh, goddess, that was rude." She covered her mouth.

Raydon took her hand from her mouth and kissed it. "Nah, it was cute. Let's get out of here before mayhem starts. I have a feeling there might be a riot, or a fight, both probably."

They made it to the door just as the sound of shattering glass was heard. River placed Sky behind him, looking to see what was going on. Jett launched himself over the bar, taking down a human male in a smooth and quick move like a professional football player would. The bar fell quiet and still as Jett hauled the man to his feet. "You don't ever break shit in my bar. You want to bull up, come at me with your fist. Toss a bottle across a crowded bar again and I'll shove said bottle, bro-ken or not, so far up your ass you'll be singing soprano and begging someone to pull the fucking cord, and I don't mean like on Flashdance, fucker."

"Where's all the hot waitresses at, asshole? We don't come here to see a bunch of roid rage, tatted up, biker wannabes," the guy spat.

Jett gave the guy a shake, laughing in his face. "Really, you accusing me of roid use, when you reek of the shit? Get the fuck out of my bar and don't come back." He let the man who was about twenty pounds heavier than himself, drop to the ground.

Raydon and Sky moved outside, waiting for him while he kept an eye on what was happening inside. Jett stood with his arms crossed next to Torq, while roid boy and his friends grabbed their coats and headed toward the door. "*Rye, get Sky away from the door, asshole and his buddies are coming out.*"

His twin didn't respond, but he watched through their link as Raydon and Sky walked around toward the back of the bar. "*Who's out back?*" he asked Jett through their pack link.

Jett named a couple of pack members that had him relaxing, while he followed the men outside. He'd watch as they left to make sure they didn't do anything stupid. Or at least not any stupider than throw a bottle at Jett. All three men climbed into a sedate looking sedan, probably one of their mothers, then drove off. He made a mental note of the plate number, before hurrying around back to Sky and Raydon, coming to a hard stop at the sight of his twin and Sky kissing. He cleared his throat once, then twice. "Alright, cut it out, or I'll have to demand my turn."

Sky broke away from Raydon's lips, doing that little wiggle thing that entranced him. "Your turn," she said and crooked her finger toward him.

River wasn't a stupid wolf, and never one to turn down a kiss from his mate. He eliminated the space between them, lifting her into his arms, taking what she offered and gave back just as much. Goddess, she tasted like cotton candy and spiced apples all rolled together, making his mouth water. He broke away from heaven, his breath and hers mingling. "Damn, you are truly the single most delicious thing on Earth," he swore.

She lifted her thumb, wiping away the moisture from his lips. Before she could take away the wetness, he grabbed her wrist, sucking her finger into his mouth. A moan escaped before he released her. "Fuck, I think I might have a woody."

Sky's head jerked downward, then back up. "There's no thinking about it," she laughed.

"Come on, let's get out of here and see if we can't make her have a lady boner in the theater." Raydon's arm swept Sky away from him, but River saw the wink he tossed over his shoulder.

"Girls don't get boners, they get wetties, bro." River hurried to catch up to his two favorite people in all the world.

"Excuse me, but what is a wettie?" Sky asked, taking his hand in one of hers.

River shrugged before answering, his wolf suddenly on alert. He lifted his head, scenting the air. Raydon did the same, both of them trying to keep Sky from noticing. "A wettie, my dear, is what a female gets when her mate, or mates in your case, get you all hot and bothered and make your panties wet. Hence, a wettie."

Sky gave a very loud snort. "Where does he come up with these things? First, he says hand to dick visit, instead of jacking off, now a wettie. What's next?"

She let go of both their hands and hurried to move in front of them, turning so she was the one walking backward. Besides, I don't have any panties on to get wet," she informed them.

Twin male groans accompanied her words, each tried to pull her into their arms, but she evaded them, skipping away just as they almost touched her.

"Sky, you are a very naughty mate. Please, continue to be so." Raydon caught up to her first, his voice deeper than normal, his wolf coming closer to the surface.

She shivered at the thought of what it would be like to run with the two men in their shifted forms without fear. Never had she been allowed to run with the pack, her parents too worried Keith or one of his higher ups would decide she was theirs for the taking. Not that they'd truly cared for her safety, but that she'd no longer be a bargaining tool.

"Hey, what's wrong?" River asked, his body blocking her view of the road.

"I was just thinking how much I'd like to run with a real pack, but then memories of my old one made me...I've never been a part of a functioning pack. Not one that was truly pack oriented. With Keith, if there was a run, it was not for any purpose other than to further his goals, which usually meant someone else's suffering." A chill ran through her. "You ever hear that saying about a cold breeze that means someone just walked over your grave or something?"

When both men looked at her as if she'd lost her mind, she tried to smile and changed the subject. "So, what movie are you taking me to? By the way, I want a large popcorn and a large water, even though I know they'll charge for it, I want one in a cup with ice, so I can add some sweetener to it. I have a craving for sugar all of a sudden." Her mouth actually watered at the thought of sweets, which was weird since she normally didn't indulge.

"Hellmouth, you can have anything you want." Raydon pulled her into his side and began walking again, this time heading back toward the truck. She could feel both men's tension and hoped she hadn't done anything to upset them.

River's hand went to the back of her neck, lifting her hair up and ran his hands through it. "Have I told you how much I love this? There're so many different shades of blondes, browns, and even some pink hidden underneath. I bet that's Lula's doing." He brought a handful to his nose. "And like you, your hair smells delicious. I bet, when you get a wettie, even without panties, you'll taste delicious." He licked his lips.

River knew he was pushing Sky, but the scent of her fear and uncertainty was driving his wolf crazy. He figured getting her excited was a much better scent, until her needy sweet smell hit him, making it uncomfortable for his jeans to contain his huge erection. A hand to dick moment would be a great thing if he could slip away for a few minutes, but the look in his twin's eyes let him know Raydon would totally block any escape plans, the jackass. "You realize pay back is a beotch, right?" he asked Raydon.

Raydon's head fell back on his shoulders as a deep chuckle escaped. Sky looked from his laughing hyena of a brother to him, then back again. "Did I miss something?"

River wanted to point to the obvious bulge in his jeans, but figured if she didn't notice, he could pretend his dignity was saved, for the moment.

"You okay to drive, or you need me to drive your baby, River?" Raydon asked, laughter escaping even as his twin tried to hide it.

"Not gonna happen, you crazy ass nondriving fool. Sky, if he ever tells you he can drive my baby, he's a liar and a fat mouth. Feel me?" River shook his head, pointing to where his brother stood.

His brother stopped laughing on a dime, his eyes still watery from the mirth he couldn't contain. "That's mean, bro. I'd let you drive my rig."

"That's because your truck is a beast and built to tear shit up. Mine is...precious," he laughed, knowing his brother would take care of his vehicle but enjoyed teasing him.

Raydon leaned over and punched him in the arm. "Feel me?" he joked, dancing backward pulling Sky in front of him. "Protect me, love. Don't let the mean man hurt me."

Their female's giggle evaporated what was left of her sadness. "You two are crazy."

"River's the crazy one I'm the lovable one. That's why we're two peas in a pod our mama said." Raydon opened the door.

River lifted their mate off her feet, nuzzling her neck. "I think actions speak louder than words," he whispered next to her ear, helping Sky inside, waiting until she scooted over before climbing in after. Raydon already moved around to the passenger's side, his head lifting like he was checking traffic, but River knew he was scenting the air. Ever since they'd left Chaps, there'd been a strange sense of them being followed that came and went. If they hadn't promised Sky they'd not communicate via their twin link, he'd ask Raydon for an update. As it were, he had to wait until his brother got into the vehicle and rely on body language. Raydon got in, his hands relaxed, shoulders squared but not rigid. River released the breath he'd been holding. He rattled off the movie choices, grinning at Sky's choice. "You were fucking with us about a chick flick all along?"

"Well, a girl does need to see how you menfolk will act when they think they're gonna have to lose their man card for a couple hours. By the way, you both did remarkable. Besides, I love action movies more than chick flicks. However, don't even think of taking me to a scary movie, or I'll be in the ladies' room the entire time. The one about the clown and the red balloon still gives me nightmares. No thank you, sir."

"Good to know. River likes horror movies, but only ones that have plots and little gore. I like shoot em up ones, or ones about fast cars, and movies with lots of action. However, I will admit to watching Pretty Woman and Dirty Dancing a couple times. My man card is safe though, since it was when I was trying to impress the ladies." He winked.

"I don't think I want to know how those evenings ended," Sky growled.

Raydon reached for her hand, placing it over his heart. "Love, all those were watched with our mama. She loved to make us watch a movie with her every Sunday, and it was always lady's choice. Strangely enough, I didn't mind as long as we were all together. Family means everything to River and me. You, you're our family, too. For you, we'd walk across hot coals to see to your happiness and wellbeing."

A tear slid down her cheek at his brother's words. River wiped it away. "Haven't you figured it out yet, hellmouth? There was nothing before you? Sure, we cared for all the women we were with because we weren't monsters, but we never made promises we didn't intend to keep. Never did we get into a relationship, ever. We knew our mate was out there, somewhere, and didn't want to...well, we didn't want this. We didn't want her hurt because of something we'd done in the past. Our promise to ourselves and our future mate was made long before you came. We said we wouldn't give to another what was solely meant for our one. A single night or day couldn't be confused as forever. That was all we ever allowed ourselves, and those were few and far between. Right Rye?"

He looked over to see Raydon nod as they pulled into the theater parking lot, finding a spot at the back under a light pole. "Obviously, we're not virgins, but we're not man whores either. You can trust that you'll never run into a female that had a claim on us, love."

She took a shaky breath before nodding. "I have all these insecurities. You both deserve more than I can give you, but I can't let you go either."

Raydon unsnapped her belt, then pulled her across his lap. "What we deserve is a mate who was meant for us. That's you." He silenced her with a kiss.

River took the time to check their surroundings, allowing his wolf to push closer to the surface while Raydon had Sky occupied.

"We're gonna be late for the previews if you don't let our female go." River turned back in time to watch Raydon rest his forehead against Sky's.

"You gonna share that popcorn, or do I need to buy one for River and I?" Raydon traced Sky's swollen lips with his thumb while he talked.

Sky's purple eyes looked like shiny amethyst glass as they stared back at Raydon, then at him. "Popcorn?" she asked.

River reached over, taking her from his brother, easing her between him and the steering wheel. "Yes, that wonderful fluffy stuff with yellow liquid gold they pour over it that you said you wanted a large bucket of?" he joked as he maneuvered her out the door with him. Loathe to release her, River kept her in his arms for a second longer, then let her slide down his body, allowing her to feel the erection he couldn't, nor wouldn't, hide from her.

"Oh," she gasped. "I can...can share."

He took her hand as Raydon rounded the truck. The beep beep sound as he engaged the locks on the vehicle echoed around them. "Good to know. If my hands are busy, will you feed me some?" He waggled his eyebrows up and down.

Raydon felt the fine hairs on the back of his neck standing up, but his nose didn't pick up any other scent besides theirs and of course the others who were already inside the theater. Fuck, he remembered why he hated going to crowded places, and one of them was because there were too many scents that confused his wolf.

"I'll get our tickets if you two want to get in line for the popcorn and shit."

"Hey, popcorn and twizzlers are not shit, buster." Sky poked him in the chest.

He raised his right brow. "Ah, so you want twizzlers too, huh?"

She nodded, holding up her pointer finger. "You need salty popcorn, but you also need twizzlers for the pseudo sweet, and then the sweetened water to wash it all down." She held three fingers when she finished talking.

Raydon shuddered. "Are you a hummingbird then? I knew they liked sugar water, but humans?"

"Don't knock it 'til you try it," she quipped, a grin teasing her lips.

He groaned. "You're going to make me try it, aren't you?"

"Let's go, River, we must get our refreshments." She laughed as she began skipping with River, actually attempting to skip beside her.

Raydon gave a shake of his head while he stood behind a couple of teen boys. They kept looking back at him, then forward. He knew what they saw and didn't do anything to ease their fears. He and his twin both had dark hair and tattoos. They were what was called mirror twins, identical in every way, so when they went to get their first tattoo, they'd already agreed on what it would be. It had been a natural decision for him to get the same tattoo on his right side, while River got his on the left. From that point on, that was how they rolled, mirroring each other in most ways, but their personalities were very different. Even how they wore their jeans were somewhat mirrored. Although they were the same size, his wallet was attached to a chain that ran across his right hip and into his back right pocket. River was the opposite, going into his left. Little things like that, most wouldn't notice, but he hoped Sky would pick up on.

He felt the two teens eyes on him again, his wolf, barely kept on a leash with Sky so close, wanted to growl at them. "What's up, boys?" his voice came out a deep rumble.

Their eyes widened. "Is that your truck out there?"

Raydon gave a chuckle. "You into trucks?" he asked instead. No need to tell them the rig in question was his twins.

They nodded. "One day I'm gonna have a nice one like that. Well, maybe not as nice, but close," he amended as his friend bumped his arm.

He answered a few questions about exhaust and engines, then the two boys bought tickets to the latest horror movie. He let an older couple go in front of him, pretending to answer a call. Although he liked the two boys, he didn't want them changing their movie to his and interrupting date night with their mate. River and his damn fancy truck. If he'd went with a regular old jacked up monster truck like his, teen boys wouldn't have such a hard on for it.

With his senses open, he scanned the crowd while he made his way toward the concession stand where he found his brother and Sky, both loaded down with a tray. "Here, let me carry that for you."

"Oh, thank you. I'll take the tickets and be the official giver of them." She grinned, wiping her hands on her thighs.

His own lips turned up into a grin. "They're in my pocket. Go ahead and reach in and grab 'em. Be careful, they're flat, not round," he joked.

"Really, Rye, how old are you?" River asked, but a devious light entered his eyes. "Maybe you should check mine first, just to ensure we didn't switch spots."

Sky swatted his arm. "Hush, you were with me the entire time." Her hand came up, pointer finger extended. "Which pocket?"

Raydon thought about lying and having her go for the wrong one but then figured that wouldn't be right. He nodded downward and to the right, indicating his front right pocket. "In there, but seriously, the tickets are flat, you might have to...dig deep." He winked.

"If something jerks while I'm in there, I'll pinch it."

He bent, placing his lips next to her ear. "I get even, baby, and I promise, I'll do more than pinch, but you'll like it."

Sky's face turned a becoming pink, but she pressed her fingers into his pocket, pulling the cardstock tickets out. He really wished he'd have shoved them a little deeper. If he'd have known the sweet fingers of his mate would be so close to his cock, he'd have shoved the papers all the way to the bottom and toward the middle of his jeans.

River snorted, making him look up. The mirrored look of need reflecting in his twin's eyes let him know he wasn't the only one in need of their mate. Slow and easy wins the race, they say. Damn, he really hated slow and easy, unless it was when he was making love to Sky, then he'd take it as slow as she wanted. Fuck, the thought of her naked and in bed between him and River had his cock surging to full staff, making it a tight fit in his jeans. Never would he have thought he'd be glad to have a bucket of popcorn, until that moment, hiding his obvious arousal.

"Oh good, the previews haven't started. Want to sit in the front here, or way at the top in the back?" River asked.

Chapter Seven

Sky looked around the mostly empty theater, silently congratulating herself on the choice of movie. "Well, the most optimum place to make out is the very back, but the best viewing is right there." She pointed to the middle where there was a bar in front of the seats, preventing anyone from sitting there, yet wasn't in the very front at the bottom where it would be too close. Argh, she hated to be the one who chose. "How about rock paper scissors? If you win, it's the back. If Raydon wins, it's the front."

Raydon looked at his hands filled with popcorn and her water, then back at her. "How about we sit right down here in the middle. If you have to go to the ladies' room in the middle, you can wiggle through the bars here and one of us can maneuver out as well."

She felt the slight tension ease out of her at his statement. "How'd I get so lucky?"

"We're the lucky ones." Raydon leaned in for a quick kiss. "Come on, let's go take our seats before the lights go out." He chuckled. "Too late. Hold on to me."

Following Raydon, she kept one hand in his back pocket, so she wouldn't lose her footing as the lights went out. Even though she could see as clearly as if it was daytime, it was still nice to have a connection with the two men.

As predicted, only a few others joined them in the theater, sitting far enough away Sky didn't worry about being seen or overheard. "Thank you for...well everything. I'm still adjusting to the new me. I'm not sure what my wolf is going to be like the first time I shift." That was a huge issue in her mind. The other voice she'd effectively blocked off, but now her wolf seemed silent as well. However, she felt her dragon, or Lula's dragon part inside, yet she didn't think she could shift into one, just felt the burning sensation.

River's fingers tangled in hers, making her acutely aware she'd been plucking at her pants. "Your wolf is there, Sky, I can sense her. My wolf wants to run tonight. How about yours, Rye?"

Her eyes sought Raydon's, looking to see if he too wanted to run with her, needing to see if it was a need or want, or if it was just him being nice. "You don't have to lie. I mean I understand if you..." She stopped at the glare he wore.

"Hellmouth, first, I'll pull you over my knee if you finish that sentence. If all I wanted to do was be nice to you, I wouldn't have—we wouldn't be here now. You're our mate. We may not have marked you, or completed the bond, but you're ours. We feel it just as our wolves feel it. Tell us you don't feel it, and we'll move back. It'll be like ripping a part of our hearts out, but we'll do it. The last thing either of us want is to rush you, or hurt you, but know this." He gripped her chin in between his fingers. "Second, we'll never stop wanting you or trying to get you to feel even a smidgen of what we feel for you. You've blocked a part of yourself off. For whatever your reasons, and we felt it like a slap. River nor I have pushed for answers, but we'll be damned if we allow you to think we don't want you any way we can have you."

Hope swelled in her chest, making her wolf press forward. "Oh goddess, I'm sorry. I'm so fucked up. I do want you both, so much. I'm just...I want to be enough. I've never been enough for anyone, not even myself." There, she'd said it. Being not good enough sucked. Knowing everyone who was supposed to love you thought you weren't good enough, and told you on a regular basis, sucked. Hell, her parents would compare her to every other female in her age group, pointing out how much better they were than she was. If only she'd been a boy, or if only her twin...she cut the thought off in case it gave the other being power.

"Kiss me and I'll forgive you because you are more than enough for me and River. We'll make for damn sure you know it everyday for the rest of our lives. However, there will be...what's the word, River?" Raydon broke eye contact with her to look at River.

"You mean what's the word for what'll happen if she puts herself down?" At Raydon's nod, River moved in closer to her back as he lifted the arm that separated their seats out of the way. "Well, baby, that word and action will be a punishment. One we'll decide on as we go. So, that was your freebie. Next time, we'll have to teach you the error of your ways." His tongue licked the shell of her ear.

Sky shivered, a moan escaping. "Um, what?"

Raydon kept ahold of her face. "Depending on how bad the infraction will determine your punishment. Of course, you'll enjoy them almost as much as we will. Afterward. Now, give me my kiss so we can watch the previews, they're my favorite part of the movies."

She was having a hard time wrapping her head around their words, but one thing she knew for sure, she wanted their punishments because she knew neither man would hurt her. Her tongue swiped over her bottom lip, making Raydon groan. "River's holding me in place. I'm gonna need you to take that kiss."

"We got ourselves a brat, brother." Raydon didn't give her a chance to comment, his mouth covering her own with a masterful kiss that stole her breath and her sense of time and place. Her eyes fell shut, the feel of fingers trailing along her ribs made her shiver. Goddess, she wanted them to touch her breasts, her pussy. All three at the same time. Her men seemed to know what she wanted without her saying a word. A set of hands curved around her breasts, plucking at her nipples while another trailed between her thighs. She was most definitely getting a wettie.

The sound of the movie coming on made her jerk backward, hitting River in the nose with the back of her head. "Oh no, I'm sorry. Are you alright?" she asked in a whisper, blinking her eyes, wondering if anyone noticed the three of them making out in the front row.

"I'm fine, love. My cock is hard as a rock and my ego is bruised, but I'm good. I love the feel of your breasts in my palms. I can't wait to slide my cock between them," he groaned.

"Sssh, stop that, or I'm going to come in my jeans like a little boy," Raydon growled, shifting in his chair. He held the popcorn on his lap, the bucket half empty. "Shit, I'm going to go get this refilled before the movie starts."

Sky shook her head. "No, you love the previews. I'll go," she offered.

River laughed. "I'll go. I need to go to the little boys' room anyhow. And no, I'm not gonna have a hand to dick moment, asshole." He stood, grabbed the bucket from Raydon, then leaned down for a quick kiss. "You two behave while I'm gone."

To say he was happy to see Sky's gorgeous purple eyes shining with need as he walked away would be a total understatement. Knowing his twin was there to ensure she was taken care of was another reason he and his wolf were calm while he waited in line for a refill. A chuckle escaped him thinking of why they needed more popcorn before the movie even started.

"Piss off asshole. It's not my fault our mate has me in knots and my dick jerked too hard inside my jeans it knocked the bucket onto the floor," Raydon growled through their link.

"You're doing that twin speak our mate told us not to do," River replied, his eyes on the two boys in front of him, who seemed to be in a heated debate over which was better...Marvel or DC? Since their girl loved all things Deadpool and Iron Man in equal measures, he was team Marvel. Besides, they always had little clips at the endings whereas DC was hit and miss.

Raydon's grunt came through their link loud and clear. *"There's something I wanted to check with you about. When she was relaxed, her walls were—I don't know, less thick or high, whatever. My point is, there seemed to be another in there. It was like her, but not, then her walls came slamming back into place. Did you notice anything when you were kissing her?"*

River moved forward, placing his empty bucket on the counter. "Refill please, and can I get some twizzlers?"

The young girl blushed, hurrying away to get the popcorn. *"I didn't notice, no. I was too busy getting lost in her sweet taste. Shit, do you think it was part of Lula?"*

He could feel Raydon's mental head shake before the negative answer came through. *"Nah, this other was more like Sky, but not. Does that make sense?"*

"One of us needs to be vigilant and stay aware when we're with her. Hell, even when we're not with her. Fuck, my wolf is going crazy wanting to complete the bond between the three of us. Whoever said patience is a virtue was a dumbass," he swore.

River thanked the girl for the refill while pondering what his brother had said. They'd learned the hard way not to dismiss little things, especially if it came to Sky. No, there was no such thing as too small or out of this world to be dismissed.

A smile lit his face to find he hadn't missed the beginning of the film, his eyes scanning the small groups of people. Before he made his way toward his seat, he paused when he neared a couple seated near the middle, his senses drawn to them as if alerted by something. He tilted his head to the side, trying to figure out where he'd seen the female before, his nose picking up her shifter scent. Her eyes met his, recognition in their dark brown gaze. She sat up a little taller, her head turned left as if she knew where Sky was. She gave him a little wave, one her partner couldn't see, then settled back.

River went to his seat, determined to find out the name of the shifter girl. If she knew Sky, he'd know her as well.

"What's put that ferocious look on your face?" Sky asked, holding out her arms for the popcorn, her tone light and teasing.

Shit, his poker face must be slipping. "Hey, why do you get the popcorn and not me? What if I wanted to hand feed you while watching the movie?"

Sky laughed. "First of all, if you like your fingers, you'll give me my bucket, buddy. Second, nice try at evasion, but fail. Now, gimme, and answer the question." She wiggled her fingers at him.

He didn't and wouldn't lie to their mate, unless it was for her safety. At the moment, the little she-wolf behind them didn't appear to be a threat. Leaning closer so he could whisper into her ear, knowing Raydon would be able to hear, he explained the interaction. "Now don't go and whip your head around," he admonished, nibbling on her ear while his hand held her head in place when she tried to do just that.

"How am I to know if I know her or not?" She sounded all kinds of pissed, which made him hard. Fuck, everything made him hard when it came to Sky.

"Look into my mind and check out my memory. I tried to catalogue everything I could. If you know her, you should be able to tell from what I saw." He hoped like hell he was strong enough to hold his wolf back when their mate entered his memories. It was one thing to share a link when speaking, but to allow another into your mind, allowing them access to something personal, was on a whole other level. A slight motion, almost as if he'd just been stroked with a feather across his brow was the only indication Sky was in his mind until her presence was recognized by his wolf. While many other shifters didn't consider their wolves separate entities, he and Raydon always had a different connection with their wolves. He wasn't sure if it was a twin thing or if the others just didn't connect with their four-legged counterparts the same way they did. The wolf pressed closer to Sky's incorporal being, his joy at having her so close had the beast almost rolling onto his back with his four paws in the air, ready to beg her to pat his belly. In a matter of seconds, his beast went from happy to alert. River watched Sky sift through the memory in question, her smile quick and easily registered with recognition. The name Joni popped into his conscious mind.

He connected with Raydon as soon as Sky entered his mind, wanting his twin to witness all that happened in case he missed anything. Now, with his wolf ready to attack Sky, yet whining as he recognized his mate, River was worried. *"Calm down and let's try to figure out what the hell's going on."*

"Joni's here with Atlas?" she asked, her voice barely above a whisper.

"Is that her name? I thought I recognized her. She came to check on you a couple times when you were out of it. Taryn said she was cool, so we didn't stop her." Raydon glanced over his shoulder, his body tensing.

"Atlas isn't a wolf."

River looked at his twin, his brows raising. "Yeah, I kinda gathered that myself. Niall aware there's a bear shifter, maybe an entire clan in our territory?"

Sky sat the popcorn on the floor by her feet, placing a hand on each of their thighs. "Joni has a hard time with wolves. If she's dating or whatever with that bear, then please leave her be. If there's a clan of them, please, for me, be nice."

River glared up at the dark ceiling just as the room went dark and the movie began. "Mate, you ask a lot. We can't keep a thing like that from our alpha. We can, and we will speak to the bear in question first to see what's what, but we will be contacting Niall directly afterward."

She gave a slight squeeze to his leg. "Thank you. Let's enjoy the movie. Afterward, I'd really like to enjoy you two." Her hand trailed higher on his thigh, grazing his balls, then she released him to pick up the bucket of popcorn.

"Little tease, I hope you know you play with a wolf, you definitely will find out how big his...teeth are."

Sky turned toward him, her purple eyes glowing. "I certainly hope so," she whispered, her voice huskier than he'd ever heard before.

Raydon adjusted his dick, groaning at the constriction his jeans were giving him. Sheot, he was the one who might need to go to the public bathroom for a little relief. Hearing her whispered words nearly unmanned him. "Sky, Jeezus, girl, don't fucking say shit like that and expect us not to toss you over our shoulder."

"Oh, that sounds very cavemanish. I think I likey."

River pulled Sky's face toward him. "You alright, Sky?"

Throughout the movie she seemed more touchy feely, something he and his brother would've enjoyed immensely, but something didn't feel right. After the show, they both picked up their trash even though she was determined to distract them.

"Come on, leave it. The quicker we get home, the quicker we can fuck. Goodness, I feel like it's been forever since I've had any D."

Their female didn't refer to sex so dismissively, not to their knowledge. Hell, they'd been in her mind, seen her memories and knew for a fact she didn't think of sex as a wham bam thank you ma'am. Which begged the question of what the hell had come over Sky?

The ride back to their home was an exercise in restraint for him and River and only his brother's quick reflexes prevented them from wrecking as the female, he wasn't calling her Sky, because the vibe coming off of her wasn't that of the woman they felt was theirs, kept trying to undo their jeans. He didn't know which of them was struggling more, him or River? She wasn't quite as aggressive toward River but watching her try to undress and use her body to get him in a state of need had to be just as bad. Goddess give him strength.

Opening their link, he dismissed his promise to Sky about not using their private twin link, finding the same worry he felt reflected back at him. Sky's mind seemed to be conflicted when they tried to look into her emotions. A new wall was up, different than the one they were used to seeing. *"Does this wall look odd to you?"*

River's growl echoed through their link. *"It's darker, almost like an oil spill would look, only if I touch it with my mind, I feel the instant need to recoil. I've never had that reaction with anyone before, not even Sky. You?"*

He searched around the mystical wall, searching for any clue as to what it was or how it was formed. A slight fissure in the corner pulled him toward it. He could see the wall he'd seen before hidden behind the oil slick one. *"River, come here. I think our girl's been hijacked and is now being blocked. Look at this."*

His twin's mind joined his, the anger rolling off him added to his own. *"Let's get this fucker out of our mate."*

"I'm all for that, but how do we do it?" River asked.

"Slide between the crack here and find our girl and make her do it. She's tougher than whoever is pretending to be her."

"You know, I like it better when you tell me to slide between cracks that are real and...I'll just stop now while I'm ahead," River agreed.

Raydon lead the way, easing his mind between the small crack, hoping like hell it went where he hoped it would and that was to their not yet claimed mate. Once they kicked the intruder out, he and River would convince her they were the men for her. Goddess, he prayed she was okay.

Once through the crack, he found the space that was almost as familiar to him as his own mind...a complete chaos. *"Sky,"* he called out.

"Look," River whispered.

"*Holy shit,*" Raydon growled as he saw what his twin pointed out. Off to the side, near what would be considered the back of someone's mind was a huddled form. Their Sky was rocking back and forth, her hair covering her naked form. What the hell had caused her to retreat inside her own mind, and who was the imposter pretending to be her? "*Hellmouth, what's wrong?*"

Sky's head turned from where it lay on her knees, her purple eyes dull. "*I can't get out. She's locked me in. You're not really here either.*" Her head turned back toward her knees.

It had taken all his control not to demand the female touching him inside his truck to back the fuck up. He'd looked into Sky's amethyst eyes, wanting to see her looking at him with the desire the body was showing, but it wasn't her—exactly. Oh, it was her body, her eyes, but not her running the show or hands. Fuck, the demanding hands had nearly had his wolf snapping out of his skin. Shit, his beast was never one to hurt a female, but he wanted Sky and only Sky. The being taking up residence in their female was not Sky. Of that, he was 100 percent sure.

He snapped back to the present at Raydon's growled words, where he crouched next to the cowering figure of Sky. Even in her own mind, she was little more than the female they'd found all those months ago after the bastard had almost killed her. They'd both sworn to love and protect her, with their lives. "*We suck at protecting our female, bro.*"

In slow measured movements so as not to scare Sky, he too got down on his knees next to Raydon, lifting his hand slowly. "*Sky, this is your mind, your body. Nobody can lock you in or out. You're stronger than her, or whatever that being is,*" he tried to reassure her.

Sky shook her head. "*She's stronger. She survived even after I killed her.*" A tear rolled down her leg, making River's heart clench.

"Sky, listen to me. If you killed anyone, they deserved it. If this bitch survived, well then, we'll just kill her again. She can't have you or your body. You're ours, and we take care of ours. To get you, she'll have to go through both of us, and we sure as fuck don't want her. You're our mate, unclaimed or not. Now, get your shit together, and let's get that bitch out of here." Raydon waved his arm in an arc, his tone authoritative, gentling it at the end when Sky jerked.

She lifted her head, finally meeting his and then Raydon's stares. *"You don't understand. She was my twin, but I killed her before she could be born. All this time, she's survived on another plane. Imagine the things she's had to...endure. All because of me and my selfishness, even as a baby,"* she hiccupped a cry.

River stared over at his twin, then back to Sky. *"Love, let me tell you a secret. See that ugly bastard over there?"* He pointed to Raydon, waiting until she looked back at him. *"We were in the womb together, but I have no recollection of that time. How 'bout you, Rye?"*

Raydon shook his head. *"Sky, babies don't have a nefarious bone in their tiny little bodies, especially ones in their mother's womb. Whatever that being has said, she or it is full of shit."*

"Start from the beginning and how you know who this female is and how you know she's telling the truth." River tried to keep his tone neutral yet forced authority out. Sky was usually dominate with the infusion of Lula in her DNA. However, she was truly a bit broken.

"She's a chimera. I don't know how or why, but somehow, she reconnected with me the other day. I felt a weird burning sensation. At first, I thought it was a dragon thing with half my body turning beet red. Then, I felt a stirring in my mind, followed by her voice. She told me...told me about her death and how she'd been waiting for a chance to come back. I built a wall in my mind to block her and her thoughts and tried to contact Lula, but she just keeps getting stronger somehow. When you opened your mind to show me your memories it was like a switch was turned on, or off.

I heard her laughter. It was what you'd hear when a psycho was actually on the loose. Shit, that's exactly what happened." Sky shuddered.

River sat down, pulling Sky onto his lap. *"What happened next?"*

"She told me she was going to claim my mates that I was too scared to claim, then she'd claim my pack and take over the dragon. I don't even know what the hell that means. I know Lula gave me a part of her to save me, but I don't feel a dragon in me. I'm pretty sure if I could shift into a dragon I'd do it in a heartbeat." Her eyes narrowed, voice turning into a deep growl. *"She's not claiming what's mine."*

Raydon smiled. *"Damn right she's not. We're yours, not some chimera's. First, we need to force her either out of you or behind that wall you created. Then, we need to get in touch with Lula. Whoever this is, she might be from her world, or some fucked up place. Either option isn't one we want to fuck with. We just got you, and neither River nor I will do anything to harm you."*

"I want you both so much. I was hoping after the movie we could've come home, and...well I was hoping you both would've realized I wasn't this damaged female you had to wear kid gloves with anymore. Yet, here I am, cowering inside my head, needing to be saved again. Fuck me, I need to grow a set of balls," she growled.

River laughed. *"I think I speak for both Rye and I, when I say; we really don't want you to have balls."*

She punched his chest lightly. *"Figuratively speaking. A set of lady balls like Jenna or Taryn. I don't like feeling like a weakling."*

Rubbing his chest where she'd punched him, he grabbed her hand. *"Love, you don't punch like a weakling. You just need to find your strength and keep it. We, your mates, will help you, but you can't lock us out. Keeping secrets is dangerous. For this, our mating to work, we need you to trust us. Can you do that?"*

Chapter Eight

Sky took a shaky breath, knowing her next words were going to make or break her relationship with River and Raydon. *"I trust you with all of me."*

Air whooshed out of the male beneath her while the other twin reached over, plucking her from River. *"Damn right you do. We'll never give you a reason not to, either. We love you, hellmouth. Now, let's get this bitch out or back behind a wall so thick she'll wish she'd never tried to fuck with you. Then, you, me, and River have a mating to complete."*

She didn't get a chance to reply before Raydon covered her lips with his. If someone would've asked if she thought you could kiss in your mind, she'd have said no. Heck, she wasn't sure if she truly was kissing or if it was her imagination. Probably a mixture of both, but she was going to do all in her power to do as they said. With the strength of her soon to be mates, she knew they would win. Goddess help her, she wanted to be their mate more than she wanted her next breath and the bitch taking up residence in her mind was stopping her. A small whine from her wolf had her growling back, the sound of a dragon rumbling inside her followed, lending her strength. Oh yeah, she wasn't a weakling. *"Let's do this. I think she took advantage of me while I was focused elsewhere. I fucked up, but I won't again. Next time, I'll be sure and kick the bitch in her astral lady nuts."*

Her two men gave an exaggerated shiver each, but Raydon stood with her in his arms. *"Is this real? I mean, I know we're in my head, but what's going on outside of here? Who's guarding your bodies against me or rather shebitch?"*

River tipped her chin up to meet his lips in a sweet kiss before answering. *"Well, we had a feeling something was off about you on the way home. Our first instinct is to protect you, which means we made a call to Niall. He and Zayn met with Peyton in the driveway of our home when we got there. Having a powerful Fey is quite handy. She's handling the other, while our alpha and the second protect us and you. Trust us, we'd never leave anything up to chance when it came to you."*

"Alright, you three, I've got the other, who by the way is a nasty one, subdued. You ready to send her back to sleep until I can contact Jenna? She's going to need to open a way to another realm or we need another body to put her in before we dispose of her. Yes, it's a her. I'll explain more once you're out of there. Now, let's hurry this along, shall we?" Peyton asked. She was a Fey who'd mated with the old alpha of the Mystic Pack and had power none of the shifters had. Her daughter had been the first mate to Niall before her death, leaving behind a son named Nolan who Peyton and her mate Emerson worshipped like two doting grandparents should. Her loyalty would always lay with the pack.

"You lead and we'll follow, Peyton," River said.

"Will this hurt River or Raydon? Should they leave my fucked up mind first?"

"Hellmouth, you best just hush before I put you over my knee in your mind, and then once we're out, I'll do the same in our physical bodies," Raydon promised.

"Have you noticed that when she's more confident, her potty mouth comes out?" River asked.

Raydon grunted, but Sky could hear he wasn't angry. If they didn't have what was probably an audience, she might've pushed him to see just what it felt like to have him put her over his knee.

"Ah, hellmouth, you'll find out soon enough." Raydon's eyes flashed, a promise in their depths.

"Oh lord, I'm so going to stop projecting one day." Her grin came quickly, then disappeared. *"Okay, Peyton, we're ready."* Goddess, she was more than ready to be back in control. Although, the thought of killing her twin, again, didn't feel right. Damn, she'd think about the ramification and solution to her situation later.

Following the instructions Peyton gave them, Sky and the twins eased through the fissure in her mind. The slick oily feel had her almost recoiling backward. The other female's memories flowed into her, but Sky pushed them into the corner, blocking them until she had time and energy to investigate. Blue eyes blinked back at her, eyes that she used to have. *"You shouldn't have done that."*

"Done what, escape from my own mind? No, you shouldn't have tried to take over. Now, it's you who needs to go back where you came from, or back behind the wall. This is my body, my soul, not yours." Sky grasped at the energy Peyton lent her, using it like a whip, circling the other entity. Seeing the shock, then anger flash, she didn't waste time on more words, only cracked the whip like instructed and launched the chimera back where she should've stayed. Raydon and River were there, building her wall back up, adding their strength alongside her own. Peyton's magic sizzled through her, showing her how to ward her mind. The dragon she knew had been waiting inside slid beside her wolf, both beasts crouched and waiting. Once the wall was more secure than ever, she released Peyton's magic, the beautiful gold dissipating into the air, leaving her exhausted.

"Come on, hellmouth, let's get out of here." River nodded toward the two beasts.

"Sounds solid to me," she agreed, then slipped into a deep sleep but knew she was no longer locked inside her own head. The feel of soft linen and a warm body behind let her know she'd made it out and was being tucked into bed.

Raydon stared down at Sky and River. They'd agreed one of them would stay with her while she slept, and he'd lost the toss up, dammit. *"Let me know when she wakes, if I'm not in here,"* he growled.

River didn't answer out loud, only lifted a hand before putting it back on their mates' stomach. Fuck, what he wouldn't give to say screw it and climb in beside them, but he had people in the living room, waiting for news.

He shut the door behind him, making his way into the living area, stopping off in the kitchen for a beer. The way he was feeling, a bottle of whiskey would be better. "Anyone else want a beer?" he hollered.

Grabbing three longnecks after Zayn and Niall requested one each, he popped the caps off, then carried them into the room. Niall stood by the fireplace, one booted foot resting near the hearth while he stared into the flames. His brother stood near the floor to ceiling windows that overlooked the front of the house, his back to the room. Both men were tense, while Peyton sat on the couch, almost serene with her mate, the old alpha Emerson beside her. Hell, he hadn't even known the older wolf had arrived. "Thanks for coming, Emerson. Can I get you a drink?"

Sure, he'd already asked, but damned if he wouldn't again. Manners didn't go away just because shit was going sideways.

"No, thank you, son. Have a seat, all of you. Having you all standing around growling is making Peyton tense. I can't have that, so sit, and calm yourselves," Emerson ordered.

Peyton patted his hand. "I think it's my mate you're making tense, but let's all just sit to be nice. How's Sky feeling?" she asked.

Raydon sat down in his recliner, waiting until Niall took the other, the one his twin usually sat in. Zayn walked over and sat near the fireplace on the built-in stone bench that ran along the front. "She's resting. Not hiding inside her mind, or whatever was happening." He wasn't sure how to explain what had occurred.

"From what I can tell, she'd been overtaken by a chimera. Do you know what that is?" Peyton looked at him as if she was expecting him to know the answers.

Zayn raised his hand. "A Ky whata?"

Peyton grinned. "Chimera pronounced Chi with a long I and Mira, kinda like mirror, only with an a at the end instead of the or. Make sense?"

"Hell no. None of this makes sense, but go ahead anyway." Niall waved a hand.

"It's believed that a chimera is a twin that dies in the womb. Said twin is then absorbed by the surviving twin. Most who have a chimera never know. Others have said they've felt another inside them, some have had manifestations of the twin, like a yin and yang body. One side looking different than the other. Has Sky said anything of the kind?"

Raydon sat forward. "She said everything was normal until the other day when she felt a burning sensation. That was when she noticed her body took on a red discoloration on one side. It didn't spread to her face so neither River nor I noticed."

Peyton nodded. "Something triggered the chimera, giving it life. This being may not even be a true manifestation of Sky, but a parasite from another, taking on the role of Sky's twin. Do we know if she'd been a multiple?"

"Sky said her parents were never real loving toward her, nor did they have the type of relationship where they'd share such intimate things. Niall, you could alpha order them to answer?" he asked.

Niall sat with his elbows on his legs, his head hanging forward. He turned slightly. "I'm contacting them now. Give me a moment. Since they're new to the pack, it's not the same as one of my...own."

Raydon wondered if that meant her parents weren't cooperating. Time seemed to drag on while they waited, then Niall's head came up, the alpha blue glowing. "Her parents should've been put down with their alpha," he growled. "Yes, Sky was a twin. During the last month of pregnancy, the other twin stopped moving. The mother blames Sky because she was the weaker twin and said the other baby was trying to give her more in order for Sky to survive. Babies don't have that kind of fucking power, the stupid..." Niall stopped, getting up from the chair with a low growl. "The female had to deliver both babies, but only wanted to care for the other child. I saw through her memories her disdain for Sky, and the feelings she had toward her living daughter were less than loving. I'm surprised young Sky survived that first night since both mother and father left her completely unattended, while they mourned or did whatever. I can't see what happened as their minds went dark."

He'd never felt rage the way he did in that moment. If Niall hadn't appeared next to him, he was sure he'd have been out his door and at Sky's parents' home, ridding the world of their sorry asses. "So, this bitch who took over my Sky, could it be their other daughter?"

"I'd like to discuss with Jenna the possibility and to let her follow the essence I was able to trace. From all appearances, the answer is yes. I'm not sure what deal those people made on the day Sky was born, but knowing what I do, there's a chance the other was sent to a place where she could survive and was waiting for her chance to return here." Peyton took a deep breath. "I've felt lots of evil in my life, but that one," she sighed, tilting her head toward the hall leading toward where Sky was before continuing. "She was on another level. If she'd once been one of us, she's no longer."

Raydon understood what she meant. The oily wall and feeling he got when she'd looked at him reminded him of a reptile of some kind. Not a beautiful dragon like Lula, but a slithering snake type, that would just as soon crush its victims in its tight embrace than swallow it whole for dinner. "Until we can get Jenna here, what do you suggest?" His entire being vibrated with the need to destroy anything and anyone that threatened Sky.

The feel of smooth fingers lifting his head had him blinking to find Peyton and Emerson standing over him. "You stay vigilant. If you have any inkling the other, her name was Stella, is out, you contact us right away."

"Sky and Stella," he said, wondering why they'd given them names that were meaningful. "Wait, they named Sky just that, but Stella means star, correct? Do you think that has some twisted meaning in and of itself?"

Niall stood, shrugging. "From what I could get out of them, they were always planning to name them such, depending on the birth order."

A little bit of worry eased out of him. He didn't need to look for hidden clues or dangers when there was a minefield inside Sky's mind. Dammit, he hoped Jenna or Lula got in touch with them sooner rather than later. Vanquishing whatever was trying to takeover Sky was their number one priority as it should be, for all. "Thanks for coming out. We'll stay alert and let you know if anything...well, if there's any change."

Niall pulled him in for a hug, resting his forehead against his. "We're pack, pack always helps one another. Don't ever think we wouldn't be here for you or your mate. You need to get with the mating, the both of you. Your wolves are unsettled." He stepped back, his hand squeezing the back of Raydon's neck before he released him.

Raydon nodded, his hand going to the back of his head where Niall's had been. "Got it. Trust me. We want that too."

"Why does everyone but me get the go ahead, while I was told to keep my dick and fangs to myself?" Zayn growled.

"On that note, I'm taking Peyton home. Good night, boys." Emerson and Peyton walked out the front door, shutting it quietly, leaving Raydon with a glaring Zayn and a laughing Niall.

"Let's see." Niall held up his hand. "The female your speaking of had just been bitten by my son, who'd been caught in a fucking trap. She thought he was a wolf cub and was in the midst of heat, which would've passed if your ass hadn't decided she was your mate. Hence, dick and fangs to yourself." Niall glared at his younger brother.

Zayn grinned. "Yeah, but now look at me, all mated and gonna be a daddy. I'm so glad I didn't listen. You need advice, Rye, come to me. That one, he's clearly no good at the giving or taking." Zayn yelped, jumping backward when Niall swiped out with one big arm.

"Boy, I will beat your ass. Come on, let's leave Rye and River to their mating or whatever. I hear my mate calling me," Niall joked.

Through their pack link, he could hear Alaina's laughter along with Cora's as they admonished their mates and threatened to make them both sleep in the dog houses. "Seriously, you have the full support of any and all of the pack. Whatever you need, you only have to ask. Don't try to go all cowboys on us." Niall pulled him in for another hug.

Being a shifter, they were affectionate, needing touch almost as much as they needed air. "I will. River and I would do anything to protect Sky." Neither of them would put her safety above their pride.

Niall and Zayn left, taking their alpha presence with them. He picked up the empty bottles, tidying up before making his way back to the master suite. He and River had bought the home for a few reasons, one it was close to the rest of the pack, the second, it had technically two master suites. The one they had Sky in was the one they'd remodeled and prepared first with plans to do the same with the other. Although they'd thought the chance of sharing a mate was high, when neither had truly fell for the same woman, they'd almost given up hope, until Sky. Just the thought of her sweet cotton candy and spiced apple scent had him moving quicker, until he was beside the bed, staring down at her sleeping form.

He turned to head to the bathroom, thinking he should shower and maybe take care of himself before climbing in, possibly scaring the ever-loving fuck outta their female with his raging hard on, but then her eyes opened, pinning him in place.

"Hey, where you going?" she asked, blinking up at him.

Her beautiful purple eyes were his undoing. No shower for him. He'd just lay down and hold her through the night. He could do it. With a nod, he bent. "You need anything before I lay down?"

She lifted the blanket, one silky thigh appeared. "Nope, just my two guys safe next to me."

Fuuuck, he was going to need to count backward or some shit to make it through the coming hours. Easing next to her, the bed barely moved under his weight thanks to the mattress that had cost them a mint. "You're safe with us, Sky," he promised.

Her legs rubbed together, making his jeans feel even tighter. Christ on a cracker, he needed to think of anything other than how sexy she was.

"Kiss me, Rye," she asked.

He nodded, leaning over her and took her lips in a kiss that stole his breath. Fuck, he wasn't a poetic man, but damn, he could understand why some men were. Pulling back, he nibbled on her lower lip, making her squeak as his hand found its way toward her breast, squeezing the nipple. "Damn, you're so fucking beautiful. Beautiful and wet. I can smell you, Sky, and it's making me fucking hungry. Can I taste you?"

Her legs shifted again, but she nodded. He moved, kneeling on the end of the bed, only to change his mind. River sat up, a smile lighting his twin's face. Raydon ignored him as he grabbed Sky by the ankles and pulled her down toward him, his hands going under the T-shirt she wore, pulling the panties down and tossing them onto the floor. He let his eyes travel over her lower half. "Fucking beautiful doesn't do you justice." He knelt, letting two fingers trail along her pussy, easing inside her while River did away with the T-shirt. They were swamping her in sensation, but they wouldn't take her, not if she wasn't ready.

Her back arched, a moan filled the room. "Goddess, yes, Raydon. Put your fingers in me."

"Your wish is my command." He used her wetness to coat the two digits, inserting them into her tightness, then leaned over her, placing his hand next to her head while he fucked her with his fingers. "Take my fingers, baby, tell me how they feel." He pumped them in and out, but took her next moan into his mouth, his thumb ran over her clit making her cry out.

When he felt the first stirring of her orgasm, he moved back down, kissing and licking a trail down her slim figure until he reached her mound, then he sucked her clit into his mouth while he eased a third finger inside with the first two. Sky shouted, her back arched while her hips bucked back and forth, fucking his fingers like he told her.

Sky wanted to tell Raydon to stop, then wanted to ask for more. Goddess, she needed more, and then he was there, giving her more, lining his cock up to her entrance. "You want this?" He paused, poised over her.

She didn't know when he'd taken off his jeans, but was never happier to see both he, and River had both joined her in all her nakedness. "Yes, please, fuck me, Rye."

Raydon shook his head. "No, I'm going to make love to you, hell-mouth."

Her eyes landed on his huge, hard cock. Looking over, River had one hand on his own extremely large, and yes hard dick. "Please, make love to me Raydon and River. I want you both."

River's deep chuckle had her gaze turning to him, his lips blazed a trail over her chest, across her jaw until he was whispering in her ear. "Love, we will make love to you, there's no doubt about that. For now, let's just enjoy what happens." His fingers pinched her nipple at the same time Raydon entered her.

She whimpered at the fullness, making both men freeze.

"You okay?" Raydon asked.

"Yes, you're just...its fine," she whined as he moved out then in.

"Fuck, you're so tight. Hold on." He pulled back out, kneeling between her legs, his lips, teeth and tongue working magic as they brought her to another orgasm as he licked up and down her center, driving her insane. Her breath hitched as she crested again, "Rye, fuck me please. Make love to me, whatever you want to call it, just put your dick in me."

Raydon chuckled. "Ah, hellmouth, I'm going to enjoy so much with you. Come one more time for me," he ordered.

Sky was ready to tell him she couldn't but then River bit down on her nipple at the same time as Raydon sucked her clit into his mouth, making her world shift as her orgasm crashed over her again.

"That's it, hellmouth. Come for us," he ordered as he fucked his fingers in and out, milking her orgasm from her.

"Goddess, yes, oh shit, I'm coming," she cried out whimpering when he replaced his fingers with his cock, his entrance easier than last time.

"Sheot, I'm ready to come already," Raydon growled. "Fuck," he swore, his body moving in and out jerkily. Sky felt him come, but he continued to pump and then growled landing with his body braced on his forearms beside her head, he looked down and grinned. "Damn, that was almost perfect."

"What he means, is he was a greedy bastard. Sleep now, Sky." River said from beside her.

She looked over at his naked form, his dick still hard. "I don't think so," she murmured. "I don't know how to...do it, but I want to please you. Will you let me?"

River's eyes glowed in the darkness. "You always please me, Sky."

"That's not what I meant, and you know it. I want to suck you off. Will you let me?" She got on her knees, uncaring that she was in a begging position. She was taking control, not just giving it.

A quick glance toward Raydon showed he'd reawakened. A grin curved her lips, then River gave a deep rumbling growl as he moved back until he was leaning against the headboard. "Come here, Sky," he said hoarsely.

Slowly, she crawled to where he reclined. Goddess, how big was the bed? She could feel two sets of identical eyes on her, watching her body as she moved, could feel their heated stare on every movement she made, each sway of her breasts.

"Damn, her ass looks amazing from here," Rye stated, need in his voice.

Sky dug her nails into the sheets beneath her, wetness coating her thighs, a mixture of her and Raydon's essence. "You look pretty fine to me, too," she said once she was next to his legs near his cock. Close but not touching.

"Put your hand around me, stroke my cock with your right hand, love." He showed her the pressure he liked.

Goddess, his dick was as big as Raydon's. Hard as steel and pulsing in her hand.

"Squeeze it, gently, then rub your thumb over the tip. See that come, you've got me ready to blow just from your soft touch," he groaned.

Sky spread the pearly white fluid over the head, then leaned forward, locking her eyes with his as she took him into her mouth. River growled, his hands fisting in her hair, but he didn't take control, his fingers combed through, massaging, encouraging her.

Twin moans filled the room, making every cell in her being filled with the need and want to please River, knowing Raydon would feel, through their link, the same thing. She wanted to please them both, wanted to make them happy, not just because she wanted to stay with them, although she did want to, but because she loved them. Her heart soared at the knowledge that it wasn't just her wolf that wanted them, but she did. The Goddess had given her two men, a gift she would treasure.

She slid her tongue over River's cock, opening the link between the three of them, letting both men feel her emotions, wanting them to know how she truly felt. Twin jolts of emotion filled her, shooting love through their link. She stroked her hand up and down at the same time as she sucked and licked, paying close attention to every moan and muscle spasm, learning what he enjoyed and what would push him over.

"Take me, as much as you can, Sky."

His words had her on the edge of coming herself, then Raydon's fingers were there, sliding between her folds. She did as they told her, letting his cock go as far back as she could until he hit the back of her throat, loving the shudder that wracked his big frame.

"Squeeze my balls, too," he moaned.

Sky trailed her tongue back toward the tip, repeating the action while she massaged his balls, licking his cock and swirling her tongue back and forth along the tip.

"Fuck, I'm going to come."

She pumped her hand up and down, barely able to concentrate as Rye worked between her thighs. With every moan and groan River gave, she was driven to work him to orgasm before her own.

"Goddess, Sky," River said on a groan. "That's it, keep doing that, love. Yes, just like that."

The pleasure she got from sucking River made her wetter. She felt his cock jerk, and then Rye was sliding into her at the same time as River's seed exploded from him, his hand fisted in her hair, holding her in place, but he didn't force her to take more than she could. The three of them were coming together, and she loved it, but wanted more. The feel of Rye's teeth grazing her shoulder had her shifting slightly. *"Do it,"* she whispered through their link.

She worked to swallow all that River offered, before lifting so she could look over her shoulder. "Please," she whispered, pushing backward. "Both of you, claim me."

Chapter Nine

River met his brother's eyes and nodded. "Do it."

As soon as Raydon's teeth sunk into Sky, they fell forward, her body falling on top of his, sandwiching her between them, her teeth sinking into his neck, marking him at the same time as Raydon claimed her. Once Raydon licked her neck, his twin pulled out of her neck and body, rolling to the side, making room for River. He quickly slid into Sky's warm embrace, claiming her body with his own, staring down into her gorgeous eyes while he made love to her. He too felt the need to claim her. His wolf rose, sinking his teeth into the opposite side of her neck, his cock jerked inside her, sealing their claiming. Licking over the bite, he felt complete, but knew Raydon would want the claiming bite he had as well. A small selfish part of him wanted to take more time, but he reminded himself they had the rest of their lives. Her hand came up, running along his jaw. "I love you both, so very much."

His heart soared at her words. They'd felt it through their link but hearing it filled him with warmth. "Love you too, so very much." He kissed her, felt his balls tighten around her pussy as she milked him, his orgasm crashing over him, consuming him. "Sky."

He rolled allowing Raydon to lift her over him, watching as his brother's lips claimed hers, then their bodies were moving together, and his kisses were hard, and their shouts filled the room. This was what they'd wanted, what they'd been missing. Their wicked little mate completed them.

River waited until they were finished, before he lifted Sky into his arms, taking her into the large master bath. Yes, they could shift and then shift again and be clean, but he and Raydon wanted to take care of their mate properly.

"Anytime we'd thought of our mate, she'd been a shadowy figure. Now, seeing you here, I can't believe how lucky we are." River kissed Sky's brow. "Come on, let's get you clean. We'll sleep in tomorrow."

Raydon grunted, but he'd already started the huge tub, the fresh scent of mint filled the air.

"Is this how it's always going to be with you two?" Sky asked around a yawn.

"Of course. You're our mate. We take care of our own." He slid her inside the tub, sliding in behind her.

"Already?" she asked looking at River and his dick.

"Hey, it's your fault. Just ignore him though."

She laughed. "You going to have a hand to dick meeting while I watch?"

He ran his hand up and down, seeing the interest in her stare. "Baby, if I had a hand to dick moment every time I got hard thinking of you, I'd be in a world of trouble, or my right arm would be huge."

She tilted her head to the side. "Huh?"

"This state here?" This is what you do to me. I'm always hard when I think of you." He released his dick on a groan as she stood up, bubbles playing peekaboo with her body.

"Come here, River," she said holding her hands out.

River slid into the tub opposite Raydon, then groaned as she slid down his cock, taking him inside. "Fuck, you're gonna kill me."

"No, I'm going to make love to you."

The water sloshed as Raydon moved behind her. "I'm gonna just play, ignore me."

Sky groaned, but River knew his twin was doing a little more than playing as Sky's body began moving faster. "Ah fuck, you feel so good, too good. Fuck, Sky."

"Now who's the hellmouth? Oh, fuck, yes, right there. What're you doing, Raydon?"

"Getting you ready, hellmouth. Not tonight, but soon, you'll take both of us at the same time," he promised.

And just like that, her body tightened like a vice, making his own come. "Fuck, yes," he roared.

The next morning Raydon was in the kitchen, his mind thinking through the previous night. Hell, his dick twitched wanting to sink back inside Sky's tight pussy or mouth. Many men, shifters, wanted their mate to be untouched by another, but he and River had never thought that way. Now, to know they'd be the last ones, that was another story.

"Wow, it got cold overnight. Where's Sky?" River came in the backdoor, his boots covered in snow. "Sky still in the bathroom? Want me to see what's taking her so long?" River asked as he took off his shoes and coat. They may be shifters, but that didn't mean they didn't wear winter gear.

"Hold your horses, boys. I was talking with Lula, kinda. She's...something." Sky skipped into the kitchen, her cheeks turning a rosy hue.

"Lula is a female who's a bit...different, that's for sure. How're you feeling this morning?" River asked, his arms going around Sky.

Raydon poured her a cup of coffee and waited his turn.

"I'm good. I just needed a minute to digest everything. I um...well, when we claimed each other, did you guys see my past?" She lifted the cup to her lips and looked at Raydon.

He paused with his own cup halfway to his lips. Fuck, he'd been so wrapped up in her pleasure and not fucking up, he didn't look past the moment they were in. Taking a fortifying sip, he placed the mug next to his hip and waited.

"Sorry, love, I was a little distracted," River confessed.

Raydon moved closer, tipping her chin up to meet his eyes. "You want to tell us, or want us to look for ourselves? Now that we're mated properly we can, just as you can. Nothing about our past or yours will change how we feel about you, hellmouth." His thumb moved back and forth over her slightly swollen lips, a sign she'd been chewing on them out of misguided fear. "Sky, whatever it is, we'll love you no matter what."

Tears pooled in her beautiful eyes, making them even more vibrant. "My parents never loved me, did they?"

He took a shaky breath realizing it wasn't her memory she was referring to, but the conversation Niall had with her parents, the one their alpha shared with him and his brother. "I could lie to you, but you saw. I'm sorry, love. They didn't deserve a beautiful child such as you."

She shook her head. "They were hurting. I was a reminder of their loss and..."

Raydon stopped her flow of words, his wolf growling and needing to end their mate's hurt the only way they knew how, a kiss meant to heal. Her tongue met his, her slim arms wrapped around him, their strength that of her wolf and dragon combined. Had he been human, she'd have cracked a rib or two. When he pulled back, they were both breathing hard. "Sky, I need you to listen to me, and truly hear what I'm about to say. Your parents are fucked in the head. They did something the night of your birth. That's the million dollar question, and we need Lula to find out, or Jenna, but it seems the Fey Queen is still out of commission since the birth of her babies."

"Lula said she'd be here in a jiffy, which I don't think she truly understands means sooner rather than later, 'cause she said something about peanut butter." A small grin tilted her lips.

Raydon imagined the female with long pink hair holding a jar of peanut butter and a spoon. "I can see it. Her popping in with a spoon in one hand while she shakes her fist holding the offending stuff in the other. I imagine she is either loving it or hating it." He himself hated the shit, but River loved it. Yin and Yang, he thought, and immediately their problem came swirling to the front of his mind.

"I caught that, too. So, Peyton thinks my twin really is a chimera?" He could hear the sadness as she spoke.

River moved behind Sky, wrapping his arms around her, making her shiver. "Just because this other being may have once been your sister, doesn't mean it still is. In fact, I don't believe it is. Once a being is no longer living, and their soul is sent to another plane, they become twisted into something else entirely."

"Stella, her name is or was to be Stella. Why didn't they go to the hospital?" she questioned.

Raydon sighed, knowing she needed to vent and ask these questions without really wanting either of them to answer. However, River was there with words, words he felt. "Your alpha was an archaic male. Keith more than likely didn't believe in such things or didn't allow useless expenses. Hell, maybe your mother didn't realize there was a problem until it was too late. Whatever happened, you are not to blame. You, like every other child, are not to blame for what happens when they are in a mother's womb. The fault lies with nature."

Not liking the stiffness in Sky's body, Raydon grabbed her from River, placing her on the counter after clearing the space. "Listen, we can argue back and forth all day and night for eternity, but the reality is that you're here and she's, well, she's locked away in your mind for now. She doesn't have a body here on Earth, yet. Did you see what Peyton suggested?"

At Sky's nod, he continued. "What do you think of her plan?"

"To bring her into this world, only to kill her seems...I don't think I could do it or allow anyone else to." She looked at him then River. "I love you, both of you. I want to be the female you deserve, but on this I can't budge."

He and River stood so close to Sky, their legs bumped hers. "I think Raydon and I knew that. Let's not worry about any bullshit. For now, we've got a mating to celebrate. Plus, I imagine you're hungry. We can throw something together or head up to the lodge for breakfast."

Sky's face showed every emotion, which he thought was a damn good thing since she was closed lipped unless she was cursing. Finally, after a minute or two of silence, she nodded. "Does everyone there know what happened?"

"Dammit, you don't think we'd allow gossip to flow about you, do you?" River growled.

Sky pushed him back with a hard shove, their feisty little female showing she wasn't such a pushover. "Listen, I'm just catching up, and I didn't quite take the time to roam your minds, so excuse me while I ask stupid damn questions, but could you please answer them?"

"And just like that, I'm hard. Can we skip eating breakfast and go have dessert? Nekkid, with you riding my face?" He held his hands up near his chin, his goofy grin in place.

"Dear goddess, tell me I don't look that stupid?" Raydon shoved River out of the way, getting in Sky's face. "Let's get a few things straight before this one decides to forego food for pussy, which by the way tastes fucking awesome." He winked at Sky. "The other employees at the lodge know what we told them, thanks to a little Fey magic. Nobody but us and a few others were witness to what really happened, and none of it was your fault, period. Even if the entire world knew, anyone with a lick of sense wouldn't think it was your fault. Look through my memories, see for yourself what happened. I can stand here and talk 'til I'm blue in the face, but you and I both know you need to see it." He spread her legs and moved in close, resting his forehead against hers, not that they needed the physical connection for her to see his memories, but because he and his wolf needed to touch her.

The whisper like feel of her presence soothed the jagged edges he'd had since they'd found her injured and near death. A familiar presence eased along with Sky's in his mind, flowing through memories quicker than he'd have felt comfortable with if it hadn't been his brother and his mate. He kept his eyes closed, breathing in her unique scent and keeping attuned to the world around them. Finally, both Sky and River left his mind, leaving behind a little bit of themselves. He opened his eyes, catching a look of hope in Sky's mind and then her intent gaze.

"So, now do you trust and believe us?" he asked.

Sky placed both hands on his face, holding him in place. "I always trusted you, and it's not that I didn't believe you, exactly. I just thought...it's that, well I thought you would try to protect me from things you thought I was too fragile for. Believe me, I'm so far from fragile it's almost comical. You've seen my memories, so now you know. I didn't grow up a pampered princess, none of us did in the compound. Keith didn't allow a female to get too big for her britches, and if one did, he made damn sure she was knocked back down, physically, mentally, and emotionally."

River growled from beside him, making his own wolf need to rise. "Sky, if we could, we'd kill that bastard ourselves. Fuck, we were so close to you all these years and had no clue. It guts us, knowing..." he bit off, pushing back to pace away. "We can't change the past, but we can make damn sure the future is better, starting now. So, let's get that fine ass up and out of here before River and I decide to say screw food and screw you instead. Your scent is driving my wolf insane with the need to dominate. It's taking all my control to tell him you need a little down time after last night."

The little vixen gave him a grin that could only be described as wicked, then she hopped off the counter. "How about we run in our fur there and come back here the same way afterward. I don't know about you, but I think that'll make our wolves happy, and maybe give them the time to get acquainted?" At the french doors leading to the back patio, she glanced over her shoulder and with a saucy wink, she lifted the borrowed T-shirt over her head, dropping it on the floor, leaving her in nothing but a pair of lacy panties. "Race you both," she challenged.

Since the Fey had gifted them with the power to shift and Jenna had shown them the way to do so without having to undress, none had needed to do so since. However, watching Sky dare them before she shifted seamlessly into an almost pure white wolf, had him rethinking the need, versus want. Hell, she leapt off the deck and into the woods faster than he could process, making the decision for him. "Last one there has to cook dinner," he said as he shifted and followed Sky, knowing River was right behind him. It would be a tossup who got to her first, both of them evenly matched.

Through the woods, he tracked her scent and easily caught up with her smaller form before they reached the lodge, her beautiful white fur blending in with the snow almost too well. He tracked the sweet smell of cotton candy and spiced apple as she dodged around a tree. His wolf came to an abrupt halt, snow spraying around him as River did the same. Sky stepped out in human form, her body dressed in a pair of black leggings and an oversized white sweater along with a pair of boots with faux fur lining.

River shifted first, whistling. "Damn, girl, how'd you do that?" he asked, walking toward Sky.

Raydon sat back, scenting the air.

"Lula gave me a crash course on all things Fey when I was with her. I told you, I may have weak moments, but I'm far from weak. That bitch in the box—" she tapped her head. "She's going to learn who's the boss of this body."

Raydon shifted, his wolf easing back to allow the human part of him to takeover. "I second what River said. Damn, Sky, I think that was one of the sexiest things I've ever heard you say. Want to skip brunch and fuck?"

Her gorgeous head tipped back, a real laugh escaping her. "Eat, run home, then make love. Sound like a plan?"

River eliminated the distance between them, bent and hauled their mate over his shoulder, slapping her rear as he headed toward the lodge. "Woman, you are a damn tease. I swear, I'm going to feast on that pretty pussy for hours," he growled.

Listening to their banter, he couldn't help but chuckle. For the next however many years, he knew he'd never grow tired of waking and sleeping as long as he had Sky and his brother with him.

River stomped his feet at the entrance, making Sky giggle as he accidentally shifted his hand between her thighs while he held her over his shoulder. Fuck, he was hard and seriously gave zero thought to who could see it. "Alright, love, I'm gonna set you down. You ready?" He didn't want to but knew he couldn't just walk around like a caveman with his prize slung over his shoulder. Plus, if he just righted Sky, she could be dizzy. He was nothing if not a gentleman.

Sky snorted. "I heard that," she whispered near his ear.

He gave her ass another firm slap for good measure, bent and kissed her soundly while putting her in front of him, uncaring that they were in the middle of the check in area. "Good. Next time I'll be sure to think dirty thoughts."

She lifted onto her tip toes. "Don't you always?"

Sassy, sexy, mate. "When it comes to you, yes," he agreed.

"Why does it feel like we've been together, the three of us, a lifetime instead of just weeks?" Sky asked, looking for Raydon.

River felt his brother enter the lodge, his twin the more serious of the two of them. "Because that's the way of mates, and the three of us have been inside each other's...minds, plus, we've been inside your delectable little body, and neither of us can wait to do it again. Let's eat so we can get on to part two of my day."

Raydon slung his arm over River's shoulder. "You'll learn his part two is really his part one. He only allows it to come second because necessity rules. Speaking of needs, I can feel your hunger. Let's go get a table." Raydon reached for her hand, steering them toward the dining room.

"One of us has to have our priorities straight. Ain't that right, love?" River held her other hand, tension had her squeezing onto both their hands like a lifeline. "Easy, nobody will do or say anything that upsets you, if they value their life."

He didn't need to look at Raydon to see his twin agreed. A human girl met them at the podium that had a sign telling them to wait to be seated. If River hadn't been head over ass in love with his mate, he might've given the girl a second look. However, he only had eyes for Sky, and his dick only stood up for their sexy mate. Which was a blessing, because if roles were reversed, he sure as fuck prayed to the goddess Sky felt the same. He'd almost hate having to kill some unlucky sonofabitch who tried to take what was theirs. Almost.

Sky snorted again, letting him know she was inside his head. "I think someone needs a timeout," she whispered.

This time is was Raydon who snorted. "That don't work. When we were kids our mama tried it. He found invisible friends to play with. Even if he could talk, you know, that was part of the timeout, no talking. He'd make hand puppets or shadow puppets. Seriously, the only thing that would bother him would be withholding food, or now you."

River gasped. "Never, don't even think to withhold my Sky Sky." He winked at the young girl leading them to the table. Oh, he knew she was probably wondering which one of them Sky was with, what with her holding both of their hands, yet here he was clearly making more of a production of her being his. Again, he gave no thought to what anyone else thought.

"Ah, there you three are. I've been looking all over Fey and Earth for you."

River froze at the sight of the gorgeous female with long pink hair coming toward them. Goddess, he still wasn't sure what to think of the dragon female, other than to maybe run the other way. Problem with that was she could fly and obviously transport anywhere she wanted. Oh, and lets not forget she's a fucking dragon. Nope, he's not forgetting any of those things.

"Uh, why would we be in Fey, Lula?" Sky asked, letting go of him and Raydon.

Lula held her hands out to her sides. "Because I was there, duh. Plus, you were calling me like elevendybillion times, so you clearly missed me. Come on, give mama Lula a hug. Oh, you too, Sky."

"You are a nut. You realize that, right?" Sky hugged the other woman, ignoring everyone else around them.

"Takes one to know one. Ps. Did you know there's a weird saying about these nuts?" Lula looked around the room. "Why's everyone staring at us. Why you all staring at us? We're not going to make out like in one of those movies, perverts." Lula winked at Raydon and River. "So, whatcha doin?"

"Would you like a booth or a table?"

Raydon had forgotten about the female. "Can we have a booth as far away from everyone else as possible?"

"He's afraid I'll embarrass him. I've told him I'm housetrained. I don't even shed a scale or anything." Lula flipped her hair over her shoulder, her arm going around the other girl with ease. "Lead the way. I'm famished. I think I could eat a horse. Not a real horse, Jenna says that's not allowed. Besides, in my human form, I couldn't stand one. I'm kinda a vegetarian, not to be confused with a pescatarian. Do you know what that is? That's when someone eats only fish. I mean they eat other non-living things. I think. I should really do some research, 'cause that is just not my thing. I can be friends with them, but our dining choices are seriously limited."

"Dear goddess, she's something out of this world, but I think I love her, like a sister. An annoying sister only we can talk bad about, but a sister," River whispered.

"She's pretty awesome, but don't piss her off. You don't want to see what happens to those she doesn't like." Sky shuddered.

"Did a horse piss her off?" River asked.

Raydon pinched the bridge of his nose, hoping like hell the answer was no. He didn't want to even contemplate the cute little pink haired female chowing down on a gorgeous stallion.

"No, horses like we have here on Earth aren't in Fey. I'll show you later if you want, or you can just go look now." Sky tapped her head, but River shook his head.

"Pass. I want to eat, and I'm pretty sure that might ruin my appetite." He shuddered comically, making Sky laugh.

"We eat fucking Bambi, why the hell would it bother you if she ate a damn horse?" Raydon asked with a growl.

River opened his mouth then shut it, then opened it again and shook his head. "That's different. We don't ride Bambi. Nobody ever had Bambi as a damn pet and like kept them in stables and all kinds of domestic shit. No, deer are food for predators. We are predators. Horses are not food for anyone. End of story, now let's go eat some damn salad or jello since my appetite is making me rethink the vegetarianism."

"That's a hard no from me," Lula said, appearing at their side, making River squeal.

"Yikes, you sound like a pig. Are you sure you're a wolf?" She cocked her pink-haired head to the side.

"Oh gawd, stop it, Lula. You're gonna make my stomach hurt," Sky laughed, her hand on her abdomen.

Lula blinked, her laser focus on Sky. "My dragon says you're not with pup."

Chapter Ten

Sky prayed the floor would open under her. "Why, that's good to know. How about we sit down where the nice lady has been standing for the last three minutes waiting for us, hmm?"

She didn't wait to see if they followed, knowing they would. Goddess, Lula was truly a little unhinged, but she was awesome like she'd told the guys.

"The menus are in the middle of the table. I'll let your waitress know you're here. If you need anything, don't hesitate to let Posey know."

Lula waited a beat, then she laughed. "Posey, who names their child such an odd name?"

Sky kicked the dragon under the table when she saw a waitress heading their way, her nametag proclaiming her as Posey didn't appear to have heard Lula, but Sky didn't want to offend the young girl. "Hi, Posey," Sky said, heading off any comment Lula might make off.

"Good almost afternoon. Can I get you something to drink while you look over the menus or are you ready to order?"

The guys placed their menus down, saying they were ready. Sky knew what she wanted, but feared Lula would be the hard one. Luckily, River and Raydon ordered first since Sky asked them to, then Lula said she'd take what they were having, making Posey raise a brow. "You want what they're both having?"

Lula crossed her arms over the top of the table. "Yes, I want to try what each are having, but would never poach on my girls' men. So, I want to order what they are, and if she orders something different, I'll take one of those, too. Oh, and I'll take the bill. I gots money."

Both guys had ordered a different variety of the largest meal with meat and potatoes, one a steak and egg and potatoes on the side, while the other a double cheeseburger deluxe with fries and a side of eggs. Lula didn't look as though she could eat even a tenth of those, but Sky knew differently. After she ordered potato soup and a salad, they waited for Posey to walk away.

"Oh, my word. Have you become a vegetarian, Sky?" Lula hugged her close. "Did these boys turn you off of meat with their Bambi talk?"

"What the hell are you talking about? I'm not a vegetarian. There's meat in the potato soup. Not much, but some. I just felt like soup. Besides, I figure I can have a little of yours..." she stopped at the low rattle coming from Lula.

"Do not even think to touch my food. I ordered it. I'm paying for it. It's mine."

"Simmer down, Lula, I won't touch your food. What's wrong, do you need to talk? Like girl talk?" Sky turned toward her friend, placing one bent knee on the bench so she could face Lula. With River and Raydon across from her, she wondered if they could feel the heat coming off of the dragon.

Lula sighed. "No, I don't need to talk. I'm just hungry and tired and a little out of sorts, but I'll be right as a dragon in no time. Now, let's not talk about me anymore. I'm here to get that beotch out of your head. My dragon doesn't like it, and neither do I."

The air seemed to freeze Sky in place. "Can you talk to that part of you in me?"

Lula waved her hand in the air. "Of course, but not like we are. It's more of a sense of understanding. It's hard to explain, but rest assured, we are working on a way to extract the soul sucker out without killing you."

"Hold up one damn minute. If there's a snowballs chance in Hell she'll be hurt, then...holy fuck, did you say soul sucker? Is that what this Stella is?" Raydon asked.

"I'm afraid so. The longer she's inside our Sky, the more she will take from her and become her. That's what they do, suck the life out of the living until they are the living. I've never seen a soul sucker out of their realm. She, whoever she is, clearly had help. For one such as they to survive in a host not of their world, they would need to be of compatible makeup. I've contacted Jenna and know what needs to be done. I promise I'll make sure Sky survives."

The waitress arrived with a tray of food followed by another girl holding another tray. They waited until all the plates were on the table before anyone spoke.

"Let's table this until we get back to our place. I want Peyton and our alpha to be present when you explain. Sky, listen to me. We don't have to do anything. Between the three of us, we can contain her." River's hand grasped hers.

Lula shook her head. "No, you can't. Once the other entity has taken over Sky, she can splinter and take over you. On this world, they can do so much damage to the humans. Think zombie apocalypse, only much better looking because they don't use up their hosts bodies and throw them away. They literally overtake them, then splinter until they've created an army of themselves. This Stella, if that's her real name, is more than likely a pawn of another."

"Wait, you said Stella could splinter and takeover. How is she a pawn, if she can and would do this? I'm not following," River questioned.

Lula lifted her fork, taking a huge bite. "Do you want me to explain it to you now, and again back at your home, River James?"

Raydon sat back, worry creasing his brow. River didn't like when the female, who acted crazy, began acting more like the adult and calling him by his full name. It reminded him of his mother when she'd gotten onto them as pups. "You're just speaking in circles. Either the bitch in her head can become hundreds or she can't. Which is it?"

Once she finished swallowing her bite, Lula set her fork down, wiped her mouth, then leaned forward. "My dragon senses the female is like you Sky, only twisted. She and you were two, but then she was no more. Her soul was given to the seekers to hold until another could give her life, but they traded her to the soul suckers. There, she found life and grew into what she is today, with the knowledge that her twin took her life. Your parents fed this to her on the night you were born. They had strong magic, dark magic, that they shouldn't have had. When I saved you, there was a little spark of her inside you. The chimera twin link. The soul suckers were able to find you through it and placed Stella's essence where it had been. Now, it's only a matter of time before they're able to overtake you. She's the gateway to here for them. My dragon essence has hidden from her and the evil that's lurking, waiting for me to return. I needed to...heal. Now, eat and we will go get 'r done." She lifted the fork and began eating, not looking back up to see how her words had affected the group.

Sky's hand covered her heart, the other clenched the spoon on the table.

River stared at Lula, then Sky. "Come here," he whispered.

The booth was large enough for the three of them on one side, but Sky had chosen to sit next to Lula. Now, with their world in tatters, Raydon was glad she listened to River. Her little body eased onto his lap, her hand reaching for his. "We can't let her do it."

"We won't, Sky. But your life is not something we are willing to throw away either. We will figure out a way to get 'r done without losing you," Raydon promised. He brought their hands to his lips, kissing her knuckles. They were so fair and unmarred next to his tatted-up ones. "You're too good for us."

"Agreed," Lula said.

Sky shook her head. "Lula, stop it."

"Hey, I was just wanting to be nice. I mean, I think I made them cry." She wiped her mouth with the napkin, sitting it next to her empty plates before she nodded at the table. "You gonna eat your food?"

River and Raydon looked at their half empty plates, then at her completely empty plates. "Seriously?" River asked.

Lula shrugged. "I was hungry. No horses in sight, so I settled for cow." She winked at Sky.

River didn't want to like the dragon, not after hearing her announce without an ounce of regret that Sky may have to die, but he had a feeling Lula was fucking with them. Or hell, maybe her delivery was fucked. Either way, Sky wasn't dying on their watch. They finished their meal with Sky sitting between them after Lula ordered some dessert, because hey, she was still hungry.

"Sky, you aren't dying today. Now, eat your food. Besides, my dragon essence that's inside of you needs the nourishment if she's to battle them suckers. Come on now, eat. Mmm, this coconut cream pie is amazeballs." Her lips sealed over another bite of the pie; the entire pie sat in front of her as if she hadn't just eaten a half a cow along with ten pounds of potatoes.

"I agree with the dragon...err Lula. You need to keep up your strength for later," Raydon agreed.

Lula made a gagging sound. "Ack, no sex talk around the children." She shoveled in another huge mouthful of pie.

"Err, I think you're older than all of us combined times like three." Sky held up her hand as she spoke and wiggled her fingers for affect.

Lula pointed her fork at Sky, then at River and Raydon. "In dragon years, you would be lots older. Wiser? No, but older. Alright, Lula is done. Let's be gone." She raised her hand, then put it down. "Shoot, I need to pay since I said I would. Hold please."

River closed his eyes and counted to five, a slight throb began to stab at his temple. "It's okay, we got this, Lula. Really, it's our treat."

The little dragon female lifted her head, a strange smile on her face. "Silly, wolfie, of course it's your treat, but I'm paying." She pulled out a black credit card. "Yoohoo, Posey, we're ready to pay. Dining and dashing is so last century."

Raydon laughed. "I really do like you, LulaBell."

Silence descended at his words, Lula leaning forward. "How do you know my full name?"

Sky shoved River out of the booth, standing quickly. "Lula, put your claws away before you scare someone. We mated fully, the three of us. They saw inside my memories," she hissed.

The long, thick, deadly looking dragon claw disappeared behind the human finger once again. "Come, let's pay at the front. Posey seems to be a bit busy."

River led the way, his brother keeping hold of Sky with Lula, the almost assuredly insane dragon behind them. He reached out to Niall and asked him to contact Peyton, wanting them all to meet them back at their house.

"Lula isn't dangerously insane. Not to those she considers her own. Sky is her own, and by mating, so are you and your brother. All the members of the Mystic Pack are under Jenna's safe keeping and as such, Lula's. I've reached out to Jenna and spoke with her mate or, Hearts Love Lucas. They've assured me, all will be fine." Niall's reassurance calmed him to a degree. However, their alpha hadn't seen this latest version of Lula. She was a bit more intense than usual.

"We'll see you at our place. Bring some alcohol. All we've got is beer, but I'm thinking we're gonna need the strong shit," he muttered.

"Trust me, you don't want the Fey laced stuff. I'm told the girls had a hangover they'll never forget," Niall laughed.

Raydon nudged him at the path back toward their house. "We shifting or walking? Lula can do her magic thing and meet us there, she said, or she can flash us all there, whichever we want."

Why Raydon wasn't contacting him on their twin link had him searching his brother for any trace as to why. "I'll leave the decision up to you and Sky. Niall and the others will meet us there shortly." He watched and waited, seeing if his news had any affect on either of the three standing around him.

"How about we rent one of the land cruisers and the four of us ride together. There's a trail that'll lead us close enough to our place I'm pretty sure we can make a trail ourselves directly to our back deck." River rubbed his hands together like he really was looking forward to riding in the all-terrain thing the lodge rented to its guests.

Lula shrugged. "Fine by me, but I just ate a whole lotta food. If you drive stupid, I'm liable to toss my food all over you."

"Guys, you think that's such a good idea. I'm not in the mood to have all that landing in my lap." Sky made a face while pointing toward Lula's belly.

"Hey, you saying I'm a bad driver? I'll have you know I can drive anything on wheels like a pro. Why, I could've been a racecar driver if I wanted. Or, if I really put my mind to it, I could've been a stunt car driver in motion pictures," River laughed.

"Come, stunter, let's go see if they have anything available. They may not even be renting them out right now since the big snow. Insurance and shit can be a bitch." Raydon put his arm around Sky, his other around Lula steering them away from his brother.

Something was definitely up. River hated not being in on the know. He spun around shocked to find Raydon leading Sky and Lula away from him. Opening the link he and Raydon shared, he came up against a block. The trio entered the lobby area, heading toward the manager's office. Sky made a whimpering sound. River's wolf growled at their mate's distress. "What the fuck, Rye?"

Lula pulled away from Raydon, taking Sky with her. "Raydon, you alright in there?"

Raydon shook his head. "What the hell we doing here?"

Before River could say a word, Lula leapt across the small space, shoving Sky toward him as she went. She took Raydon down to the ground, a shriek emanating from her making his ears ring. The next thing he knew, both Lula and Raydon were gone.

"What the hell just happened?" River asked, standing with Sky in his arms.

Sky wiggled to get down, her eyes searching the room. "Fucking sonofabitching hell. She jumped out of me into him. I didn't even feel it until Lula flashed away with Raydon."

River wanted to roar and tear shit apart. His link with Rye felt severed, something that's never happened in all his thirty years of life. One look at their mate had him pushing back his anger. "We'll figure this out. Come on, let's shift and go back home." His voice sounded almost normal, surprising since his wolf was closer to the surface, so close he could feel the beast staring at Sky, assessing her.

"I can feel Lula and the bit of dragon in me is saying she's not going to hurt Raydon, but Stella was being forced out. My blood felt on fire all of a sudden, then it was as if I could hear another voice, kind of like Lula, but not like my wolf. She took the only avenue she could and that was Raydon since he was closest. Come on, I have an idea." She grabbed River's hand, leading him back outside, running in the opposite direction to their home.

"Sky, that's not toward home."

"No, it's not, but its where all the important things happen for our pack. The sacred place of our people." She ran faster, her body outlined with a golden shimmer.

At the image, he realized the dragon was from Fey, making Sky more Fey than human now that she had part of Lula in her, unlike he and Raydon. Fuck, he wished he knew what the hell was going on.

Whatever it was, Sky was their mate and he trusted her. Whatever had been inside her was gone.

"Shift, we can get there faster if we run as wolves," he growled.

Sky nodded, then she became the beautiful white wolf that took his breath away. He too shifted, a huge black wolf next to her smaller white one. The words yin and yang popped into his head, reminding him again of the fact he and Raydon were mirror twins, while Sky had been a twin as well. Chimera, a term neither of them had heard of until now.

He kept pace with Sky, not wanting to leave her behind or let her get ahead of him. Fear for what they'd find, or who, had his wolf searching the woods they raced through. In the clearing ahead, he scented them before he saw anyone. His brother was on his back, fighting to get up, but Lula, in her human form was stirring a large pot over the fire pit.

Sky leapt ahead of him, landing behind Lula, shifting into her human form.

"Stay back, Sky. Stella wants back in you, but Raydon so kindly offered to house her while I got her out. Silly boy, courageous wolf," she muttered.

River shifted in the air, landing next to his mate, hearing what Lula said. "He offered what?" His head went to the man who looked so much like him, who was him, in so many ways.

Lula nodded. "While you were distracted with this one, he created a link with me similar to Sky's and mine. He's very good, your brother. I assume you are as well, or my girl wouldn't be mated to the two of you. Anyhoo, he came up with an idea, and I decided it was a solid plan. Now, here we are, making a nice concoction to seal the parasite in until I can get it back to her realm since someone—" she mumbled, giving Sky a sideways glance before continuing. "Not naming names, but she has blonde hair with pink in it 'cause she's cool like that, but she's stupid and won't let me just kill the beotch. So, I am now going to trap said beotch and risk life and limb to get her outta here. Ps. You're welcome."

"Lula, is it truly dangerous for you to do that? I don't, won't, risk your life for hers." Sky grabbed Lula's arm, stopping the stirring.

"Nah, I'm just messing with you. This is like a walk in the dark for me." Lula moved Sky's hand off of her.

"You mean walk in the park?" River asked.

"Why would we walk in the park?" Lula blinked purple eyes at him, reminding him of Sky.

"Release me, or you'll wish I allowed you to die when my people come and make this wasteland of humanity a true place of depravity." Raydon's voice came out with a hiss, sounding less like him and more like another being.

"Ah, aren't you a cutie patootie. Keep talking like that and I'm liable to get a lady dragon boner. Have you ever seen one of those?" Lula lifted the pot as if it weighed nothing, approaching Raydon's form without hesitation.

The being inside him must have realized she wasn't scared, allowing Raydon to surface. "Lula, what're...what're you doing? They...she, hell, I don't know who's inside me, but she says whatever you're going to do will kill the both of us." He struggled against the bindings.

Sky gasped, her hand grasping River's arm. *"They're lying to him. If there's more than one in his head, then she's opened him to more than just her presence. Lula will know what she's doing, trust her."*

"Sky, that's not just my brother, he's my twin. We've shared our entire lives. Can you honestly gamble his life on...I mean, I know Lula is powerful and all, but how do we know she can do what she says?" Fuck, he couldn't allow his brother to risk his life alone.

"Rest easy, wolfie, I'd never harm one of Jennaveve's people. Now, hush, you're giving me a tumor." Lula's voice popped into their shared link, something nobody should be able to do.

Raydon's eyes flickered, the pupils become a slit similar to a snake. "You will suffer if you do what I think you're about to do, Lula dragon." Lula waved her hand, smoke moved from the pot over Raydon. "Ah, lookie there. You trying to be all scary and all. Newsflash, snaky-poo, I've seen scary and heard scarier. A wittle sucker like you and your lot are a blip to ones such as us. Oh, did you think I came alone? Tsk tsk tsk, silly boys, you brought your C team, when we always bring our A team," she laughed, then allowed the smoke to float over Raydon, encompassing his entire frame.

"LulaBell, what did I tell you about playing with your food before eating it?"

Sky turned at the new voice behind them, barely stopping River from shoving her behind him. "That's Lula's mama. She's here to help."

"Why thank you, Sky. Nice to see you finally mated these two. Och, we need to get those parasites out of the prone one though. They're not fit for the earthbound." Belle in her smaller dragon form, walked past them, her tail flicking back and forth, making River lift Sky out of the way of the lashing tip. "Ah, wolfie, I'd not truly injure you, or especially your mate. I like you."

River noticed how she didn't say she would injure him at all, but that was a splitting of hairs, surely. A roar rent the air and then Raydon was collapsing back onto the ground.

"What the everlovingfuck was that?" he asked, trying to see around the huge dragon and Lula.

A clicking sound was his answer. "Sky, Lula needs your help. Come here quickly, but leave the wolf."

"The fuck," River argued.

Belle turned her head, huge dragon eyes blinked back at them. "You will stay where you are and not disturb us."

The second she uttered the words, he felt as if bands of steel wrapped around him. "Belle, don't you fucking do this to me."

"Silence," Belle muttered.

Sky looked back at him, mouthing the word sorry. He tried to reach her through their link but came up against a wall. Thoughts of being fooled, of what they, the dragons and the reptile like being could be doing to his brother and their mate. His wolf pushed forward, growling, forcing his way out of his skin.

"Oh my goddess, they're killing him. What do you need me to do?" Sky asked, dropping to her knees next to Raydon.

"Lula can not give anymore of herself to anyone, but you have some dragon in you. Give him some of your blood. It will save him." Belle moved her hands over Raydon's body, a writhing mass moved in and out of him, reminding her of smoke and mirrors.

"If I give him my blood and they're still in there, won't that revitalize them?"

Belle gave a roar, then pulled the two ghostly beings out. "Do it now if you want to save him," she ordered then disappeared.

Raydon gasped, his eyes opened then the color began to drain from him.

"I can give him some," Lula offered.

Sky took a closer look at Lula, seeing for the first time that the female didn't look as robust as she'd looked just hours ago. "No, he's mine." She shifted her finger, allowing a claw to form, allowing her to slice a thin line across her wrist. A growl came from behind her. River's anguish pushed at her almost breaking her focus. "Raydon, don't you leave us," she cried and lifted his head into her lap, allowing her blood to flow into his mouth. Gah, she wasn't sure what she thought of sharing blood, was glad they weren't vampires or wolpires. Just as she thought the last, Raydon sealed his lips around the wound and sucked, making her entire body light up. "Oh, fuck," she swore.

"Yeah, I think that's what the Fey Queen said." Lula moved away. "I think I'll just release, oh, good boy. Now, put those fangs away, wolfie."

Sky looked behind her, her body on fire as Raydon took her blood. "River, he's fine. Come here."

River's lips pulled back in a snarl.

"Lula, your mother blocked him from moving and speaking. Fix him," she cried.

"Jenna," Lula yelled. "Get your Fey ass out here."

"You have really gotten a potty mouth on you, LulaBell. Hello, Sky, or should I call you hellmouth like your mates? Enough, Raydon." Jenna touched his head and he released Sky. "Speak and be good, or your normal self, River. See, I'm learning." Jenna sat down next to Sky. "Ah, I've missed these woods. Doesn't it smell—" she stopped and sniffed. "Hold that thought." She got up, brushed her butt off, and spun in a slow circle. The air picked up, sparkles floating down around them. "There, now isn't that better? There's never too much glitter, I always say. Am I right?"

Raydon sat up, wrapped his arms around Sky, and breathed deeply. "So, I might've made a rash decision."

"Do you think?" Sky elbowed him.

"In his defense, I didn't think Stella, who by the way is still alive and kicking where my mother took her, even though she deserves to die but that's neither hear nor there. Anyhoo, I don't think she's truly your sister, but that's something we'll need to speak with your parents about." Lula sat next to Sky and leaned back on her arms, crossing her feet as she stared up through the trees. "Where was I? Oh, right...Stella wasn't alone when she came into you, but the parasite, aka the sucker queen, was a hitchhiker. I'm sure she has some official awesome name, but sucker beotch works for me. Your parents basically made a deal with the devil, or no, not the devil because that would be Creed's daddy and ain't nobody got time for that one."

Sky put her head on Raydon's shoulder. "Seriously, all this makes sense if you just follow the threads."

"Jenna, explain to these lesser beings. I'm exhausted," Lula said with a careless wave of her hand.

"Why yes, my dear. I shall do your bidding. Basically, Sky had two beings hiding inside her. Both were allowed the right to come back here, at a certain point in time, which was brokered by her parents at Sky's birth. I'm assuming, when Sky was near death, they thought it was the perfect time to call your sister back. In their defense, they weren't prepared to give Sky up when she was alive and well, but as you lie at deaths door, all was fair in their minds. Of course, they didn't know we'd be fixing you, or that Lula would be putting a part of herself inside Sky either. Lula, you and I need to have a talk, though, dear." Jenna got up, her hand held out to Lula.

"Ah man, am I in trouble?" Lula took Jenna's hand.

Fear skated down Sky's spine. "Do you need to do your thing and take the part of you out of me?"

River shifted from wolf to man, his steps sure and filled with so much anger she could feel it pushing at her. "No, she can't take it out of you, or you die."

Raydon jumped to his feet, swaying slightly. "Over my dead body."

Jenna held her hand up. "Everyone, calm the fuckity fuck down. You don't want me to call my bestie, or my wolpire mates, 'cause I totally will. I'm a hormonal woman whose breasts are filled with milk, and I'm feeling my babies need to be fed shortly, so just calm the fuck down," she yelled.

"Jenna, are you boobs gonna leak all over? They make bras that fix that," Lula offered.

The Fey Queen pinned Lula with her no nonsense glare. "I'm going to be the one speaking, and you four are going to listen. Lula, you're to go home to Fey and recharge. I've got healers there waiting to make sure you get what you need to be back at one hundred percent, since you seem bent on giving little nuggets of yourself to all who need, which I thank you for." A tear fell from her right eye. "Sky, you are a worthy female, who suffered much. Again, I failed you at a time that I shouldn't have."

"No you didn't. Jenna, you are not the all and powerful. My parents did this, not you. You've given us all so much, and you need to quit being so hard on yourself. Besides, you're a mother. Can you imagine doing what mine did to me, to your children?"

"Never!" Jenna's body vibrated.

Sky nodded, then found herself wrapped in Jenna's arms. "Thank you for my life, for my second chance."

"I feel different," Raydon spoke, breaking them apart.

Lula put her hand on his forehead. "That's my dragon blood, but you're not gonna have my dragon in you."

Raydon shivered. "Not that I don't love Sky and all that she is and think you're great, but I didn't want to become a wolfagon."

Jenna turned to them. "A wolfagon?"

Sky grinned. "I figured if you put a wolf and a dragon together, they'd be a wolfagon."

Lula stomped her foot. "Why not a dragolf?" She tilted her head. "I guess the other sounds better, but dragons are mightier."

"Back to the problem at hand. Your parents. If they have a door to the soul suckers, which isn't their formal name by the way, then we need to shut it down." Jenna swept her hair back and fanned her face.

The air stirred, making the hair on Sky's arms stand up. "Ah, we've got company."

"Jennaveve Cordell, what the hell do you think you're doing running off? Do you have any idea how much trouble you're in?" Lucas Cordell appeared behind Jenna, his twin striding next to him, each man holding a baby.

"What if there was danger, and the two of you brought our children in the middle of it? Bad daddies," Jenna admonished, then cooed as the little girl in Lucas's arms babbled with her arms out for her mother. The other slept soundly in Damien's arms.

Lucas snorted, passing his little bundle over to Jenna who instantly lowered her dress and began nursing the little girl. "Newsflash, my love, we know everything. Well, Ezra there said all was fine, and since our father has had him trailing you without any of us knowing, we knew you were safe. This time." He ran his hand over the baby's head, staring down at mother and child with so much love Sky had to look away.

"Beep beep, back up. Ezra is following me? Ezraaaa," she yelled, making the baby whimper. "Sssh, sorry, little one. See what you made me do, Ezra." She eyed the big vampire soldier who appeared from thin air.

"Niall is gonna shit kittens when he finds out so many strangers have invaded his territory," River growled.

"Niall already knows, and I don't shit kittens. Cordells, good to see you. Ezra, thank you for watching over Jenna." Niall nodded toward the men.

Sky raised her hand. "Can we please get back to the terrible parents who may or may not allow my wicked sister to hop back into me?"

"The chimera can only take over your soul if you are weakened. Now that you're at full strength and not allowing the connection, she can not do so. However, if your parents know of another, or if they orchestrate the death or injury of another, they can create the gateway. The only way to defeat her, your sister, is to go where she is and destroy her." Ezra pinned Sky with a hard stare.

"No, she's my twin. I can't kill her," Sky denied.

"Would you rather she return in another body and kill you or those you love? That is what will happen. She's had a taste of freedom. There's no way she'll be satisfied with life there in the Yokai Hebi Sekai Realm." Ezra kicked the dirt around where Raydon had been on the ground.

"Is that the name of the soul suckers world?" Sky asked.

Ezra nodded. "It is translated to mean The Spirit of the Snake World."

Raydon didn't want to think of what that meant for its inhabitants, or what that would imply for what had been inside his body. Hell, he wanted to shift into his wolf and take a dip into the nearest river to wash the thought of a snake slithering through him. "Does that mean they're like snake people?"

"That's where you make a mistake, thinking they have any humanity. The beings aren't human at all. Your sister, she is no longer human. Her soul went there and was consumed by them. If your parents were promised anything by them, they were lied to. The Hebi will come here and leave nothing but ruin on this world," he said softly.

"You lie. Our daughter, our beloved Stella is on the other side of the veil, waiting to be reborn. If you'd have just died, she'd be here, in your body like she should've been. Why can't you just die already?"

Sky turned at the sound of her mother's voice. "You made a pact with something worse than the devil, for what? A child who died in your womb? You want to point fingers, mother? Why don't you point them at yourself, or maybe father, or at Keith, the alpha you allowed to do whatever he wanted as long as he gave you what you wanted. Oh, don't think I don't know about your side deal with him, I know so much more than I did, thanks to my visit with your dear Stella. She was very forthcoming." Sky walked toward her parents, hatred pulsing off of them in waves.

"We did what we had to survive. You should thank us. Look at you, whoring it with two mangy wolves who are..." Sky cut her mother's words off with a vicious grip to her throat.

"I wouldn't finish that sentence if I were you. Cordell, you might want to take your children home. It might get messy around here." She didn't turn from the woman who'd given her life. The woman many said she resembled showed no sign of caring for Sky, and she knew without a doubt she would offer Sky up to the Hebi or even Satan himself, if it gave them what they wanted. "Why could you never love me? What did I ever do that was so awful? I was a baby, the same as Stella?"

Her father spat on the ground but didn't make a move toward her. "You were his. Stella was mine."

Sky froze, her fingers tightened. "That's not true." She couldn't be Keith's daughter. He was going to make her his whore. He...goddess, no. Taryn was his daughter. She'd suffered because of who she was. If Keith had known she was his, he'd have...

"You're lying," she whispered.

Nova, Sky's mother laughed. "Our mother never lies, much."

The husky voice shocked Sky, giving the other being a chance to toss Sky away.

"Nova, what the hell's going on?" Hank asked.

Sky wanted to tell her father to shut the hell up but remembered he wasn't her father, probably. "So, mommy dearest let you piggyback into her this time? How's it feel, going from my young body, to her older one?" They were shifters, and as such, her mother looked more like her older sister. However, she'd learned taunting tended to piss people off, which then made them make mistakes.

"Aw, you're cute. This, is an upgrade from the one I've been rocking for hundreds of years, sister dearest. Oh, did you forget time moves differently on other realms. So, while your puny little mind is all of twenty-five, mine is hundreds of years old. I've amassed more knowledge than you'll ever have the chance to. Now, if you'd like, we can do this the easy way."

Sky rolled her eyes. "Good goddess, someone needs to fix their lisp. Jenna, can you fix that? Or is that something she'll be stuck with?"

"Yeah, I'm afraid we can't teach old dogs new tricks. Sorry, not sorry. Now, I'm gonna need you to woop your sissy's ass so I can nurse my other nugget, mkay?"

"Ah, itsss the Fey bitch. You think you're invincible, but you're not. We will decimate this..."

"Blah blah blah, shut it snake breath. I've got babies to feed."

Sky looked over her shoulder, smiling at Jenna, which clearly was a stupid move. Her sister, mother, gah, it was hard to keep track of who was who in the land of the body snatchers, tackled her. She rolled with the female, her hand wrapping in the bun, her mother preferred, to keep her from biting Sky's throat out. "My, what big teeth you have, mother." They rolled again, coming to a stop by a pair of black loafers. Sky punched her mother in the face, wincing at the sound of crunching bone. Her dad reached for her, the movement in her peripheral had her flipping backward, losing a few strands of hair in the process.

"End this Sky," River ordered.

She winked, happy to find he and Raydon had captured her father. Her father didn't fight them, while she and the being in her mother's body circled one another.

"You know, I used to close my eyes and wish it all away. I imagined I was you with beautiful clouds hanging over me. I'd rest my head on my arms and let my thoughts take me away from where I was but then reality would intrude. Want to know about my reality, Sky Sky?"

"Would you like me to pull a violin out and play a tune for you? In Jenna's words, sorry not sorry. It wasn't my fault, you crazy bitch." She dodged left when a spear flew through the air, instinct telling her it was coming. "I used to dream I had a sister. I wanted one so badly that I imagined what she'd look like. Never did I dream she'd look like my mother though." Sky released a blast of fire, catching the being by surprise.

"Do you know there's no color in Yokai Hebi Sekai. We'd get visitors who thought they could leave, but we'd keep them just so we could see through their eyes for a time, but their colors would eventually fade to gray. If you could turn back time, would you save me Sky?"

The mesmerizing way her mother began moving had Sky freezing in place. "I...what?"

"Don't listen to her. Look at us, Sky?" River growled.

She shook off whatever the hell the snake like move was doing to her, done with talking. *"Use the dragon. We are bigger, stronger, and far superior. The snake will slither, but if you cut off its head, it will wither and die,"* Lula whispered through their link.

Shifting her hands to that of her dragon made Stella or whatever the hell it was fall back. Sky ran at the being, knowing her mother was already dead made her actions easier. She could see the green cast covering what used to be her mother's skin as the parasites had already taken over, destroying the body. With a yell, she slashed out, missing the death strike. The being fell, black blood flowing from the deep wound. "I can see the darkness in you, Sky Sky. I remember you. Do you remember me?"

The ground around them, where the blood oozed, began to wither as well. "I'll remember the mother I wished I had and the sister who never was. Goddess be with you." She raised her arm, but Ezra was there with a sword, taking over.

"You did good, Sky, but no daughter should have to take even the shell of her mother's life. Now her soul is free, and she can go to the land where light and grace awaits if she is welcomed." Ezra nodded once.

Sky had a feeling her mother wouldn't be going to the same place the good people went, but again, none of them knew the suffering she'd gone through.

"You're an abomination," Hank Matson growled, his wolf jerked from him, shredding his clothes as he launched himself at Sky.

Niall shifted, taking down the smaller wolf with his teeth around his throat. He shook him once, twice, waiting for the other man to shift back, to submit, but Sky knew her father. He wouldn't.

The growl and hatred poured from Hank as he fought their alpha, leaving Niall no other choice than to end his life.

"Don't watch." River turned so his body blocked her view while Raydon wrapped her up in his arms. Both her mates surrounded her with not only their bodies, but their love and strength.

Jenna touched her arm. "You were a mix of the three of them, so was Stella. Keith was vile and evil. Your father wanted to believe Stella was all his and Keith took pleasure in taunting him with you and his DNA in you."

"But, he...Keith, was going to...he had plans to make me one of his whores when I turned twenty-five." She gasped at the tight squeeze of Raydon's embrace.

"I want to kill that motherfucker all over again." River paced back and forth.

Sky sniffed, then looked around Raydon, relieved to see Niall and Hank were no longer in the area anymore. "Can we just go home?"

"That's a good suggestion for all of us. Sky, you're a blessing to this pack and your mates, but also to me and the goddess. Lula gifted you with a part of her, don't ever take it for granted. If you ever feel the need to speak to someone and you can't talk to your mates, reach out to one of us. We'll save you from thoughts of this blasted winter sleep. That's what this is. It's a winter sleep. Tomorrow you'll wake up and have a new day. You're still alive, with two sexy mates. Trust me, I know how lucky you are to have not one but two sexy alpha males. Take your life and live it." Jenna wrapped her arms around Sky. "Live it, Sky."

Lucas cleared his throat. "Just so you know, I've recorded that for future use. The part about being lucky."

"Lucas, you should stop before you're in the dog house." Jenna wiped the tears from under Sky's eyes. "Goddess be with you and your mating."

Before Sky could utter a word, Jenna and the other wolpires were gone, leaving her alone with her sexy mates.

"Feel like shifting and running home?" River asked.

She shook her head. "I learned a new trick."

Raydon waited alongside River.

"How about I flash us home. It'll probably drain me, and I'll need my mates to take care of me, but it'll be faster," she gasped the last as Raydon lifted her in his arms.

"Do it, hellmouth." Raydon held her to him while River stood behind her.

With the new knowledge from Lula, she flashed them outside their home, missing the inside by a few feet. "Oops, I meant to land us inside."

"This was close enough," River growled, taking her from Raydon and hurrying toward the back patio.

Yeah, it was close, but she would get closer next time.

Chapter Eleven

River carried Sky into their home, knowing Raydon was following. He'd never been more terrified in his entire life than he'd been when Sky had been fighting her mother-sister. Fuck, he was happier than all get out that Ezra offed the bitch instead of their mate. No matter how much they all knew she needed to be killed, if Sky had been the one to do it, she'd have felt remorseful. "Do you like those clothes?" he asked.

Sky shook her head. "Hate them.

He nodded. "Me too." Tossing her on the bed, he climbed over her, shredding the top with one sharp claw, then did the same to her leggings. "These panties are actually pretty nice." They were white with little snowflakes on them.

"Can you get me out of them without ruining them?" she asked.

Instead of answering, he gripped the sides, tugging them down her thighs until he could slip them off her feet. He brought them to his nose. "You smell delicious."

"I think I stink like fighting. Nasty ick." She screwed her nose up in a cute way that made him want to kiss her, so he did.

"You smell like cotton candy fresh off the spool with spiced apples mixed in. My mouth waters anytime I'm near you," Raydon growled, the bed dipping slightly as he placed a knee on it. "Tonight, we take you together," he said.

Sky glanced from his fully erect cock to Raydon's, her tongue licking over her lips like she wanted to taste them. Damn, he loved having her lips on him. Hell, having any part of her touching him was heaven. She was their living, breathing goddess. For the rest of his life, he would make it his mission to ensure she'd go to bed with a smile on her face, ensuring she'd wake with one too, or better yet, a moan escaping those pouty lips.

"You look like you're having very wicked thoughts, River." Sky blinked, her body shifted, her legs spreading slightly.

Kneeling between her thighs with the tiny panties in his fists, arousal filling the air, her words were nothing less than the truth. "Come here, Sky," he demanded.

Sky lifted to a sitting position, giving him access to her breasts. He cupped them in his palms, amazed at the perfection of her smooth flesh. He molded first one, then the other, squeezing her tiny little nipple between his thumb and forefinger, making her moan. "Fuck, I love that sound," he muttered, then took the next gasp into his mouth. He pinched both nipples, fondling them, bringing them into hardened peaks, tugging harder until he knew she was feeling the sensations straight to her clit through their bond.

He broke the kiss, pulling at the hardened buds one last time. "I never was much of a breast man, but damn, I love yours. I think it must be you. Every female before you pales in comparison."

Sky's breath came out in a rush, her fingers tightened on his biceps. "Before you two, I was lost. Now I feel as if my world stopped and started the day I woke up here, with the both of you. You make me whole, but I still feel as if I need something else to complete me."

Raydon pushed her hair back and nodded. "We understand and feel it too. Trust us, Sky. Just lie back, love."

River watched while Sky did as she'd been instructed, her head hitting the pillows behind her, her legs not quite spreading in invitation, but the look of pure want, need, and hunger undeniable on her face, which only added fuel to the raging fire in him and Raydon. Oh, their little mate didn't know the power she held over them, yet.

Raydon bent his head, taking her lips in a kiss that had her moaning.

River grinned, knowing they'd have her doing a lot more than that before the night was through. He stared down at the perfection of her pussy. Looking up he gave his brother a nod as the sweet scent of her cream coating her inner thighs made his mouth water. He laid down, wedging his shoulders between her thighs, making room for him. "Fuck, you're so damn pretty." He grazed her pussy with his thumbs, opening her up, brushing her clit with his tongue.

Sky's hand gripped his hair while she kissed Raydon, connecting the three of them, groaning, telling River she enjoyed what they were doing to her. He growled, licking up and down, over and over, teasing her clit and back down to her hole, eating at her like a starving wolf. Hell, he was starving, needing to fill her. Inserting one finger, then another, he pumped in time with the flicks of his tongue over her clit in quick rotation.

Sky began to shake, her breath coming in shallow pants while Raydon sucked her breasts. Through their link, he could feel what they were doing to her and how close she was to coming. It was all he could do to keep from doing the same.

"Oh, yes, River, don't stop," she gasped.

Raydon went back to her lips, consuming her in a hard kiss River was almost envious of, except he loved her pussy too much.

Moving his fingers in and out faster, he pressed the flat of his tongue against her clit, giving it a little rougher treatment. She gasped, her nails raked his scalp. Damn, his wolf nearly howled at their mate marking them. He chuckled, then sucked the little nub into his mouth knowing Raydon was on the edge like him. In unison, they both bit down on the flesh in their mouths, making her scream in pleasure. The blast of released tension sent waves of ecstasy through their link, making her pussy constrict around his fingers while he pumped them in and out.

When she finally relaxed back against the bed, he pulled his hand back, her juices coating him. He ran his hand over his cock. "We're going to both take you. You ready for that, hellmouth?"

A small shudder wracked their little mate's frame, but she nodded.

"River's going to take your ass, while I slide into that tight pussy. I do want your ass too, but tonight, I get your sweet pussy first, while he gets your gorgeous backside," Raydon said laying down and bringing her on top of him. "After that, do you know what happens?" he asked, guiding her onto his cock.

River ran his hand up and down his cock, coating it with her orgasm only made him harder.

Raydon watched his cock disappear inside their own personal heaven. Inside their mate was perfection in and of itself. He groaned at the feel of her wet heat kissing the tip of his dick until he was fully seated with her ass resting against his balls. "After I come inside your tight as fuck pussy, and he comes inside your ass at the same time, then I get your ass while he gets your pussy," he growled, his hips flexing just thinking about fucking her.

River moved behind them, pressing Sky down until her chest pressed onto his.

"Oh dearest goddess. You're going to make me come by just talking," Sky breathed.

"No coming until I'm buried in this pretty little hole." River's hands squeezed Sky's ass cheeks.

Whatever River was doing had Sky squirming and tightening on his cock. "Damn, River, hurry the fuck up, or I'm gonna lose control." He moved his hips a small fraction. "Her pussy's so tight I can feel her walls flexing on me already."

"Hold your shit together, man," River laughed.

"You best get to getting then, or we're gonna leave you behind," Raydon teased.

"Oh, fuck. Don't talk about that when you're...oh, you're too big," Sky cried out.

Raydon shut out his own need and focused on soothing Sky. Through their link, he felt her overwhelming fear that she couldn't take them both, instantly knowing she only needed their love and reassurance. "Sky, you were created for us. Do you know how perfect we think you are? How sexy you look, or how absolutely happy you make us? No other women in all the universe could compare to you. Once we fully join with you, you'll carry not only our mating mark, but our scents will be combined so nobody will ever doubt who you belong to."

His words seemed to calm Sky, making her body go soft. "That's it, don't tense up, love," River whispered.

Raydon palmed the back of her head, twisted her hair in his fist. "Let your muscles relax. That's right, let River in and then we'll all be in heaven."

Her slight jerk and gasp was a clear indication that River was moving steadily inside her. Her sweet pussy contracted his dick as she pushed back, wanting more.

"Fuck, Sky, you're so damn tight. Relax a little more. Ah, good, just like that," River whispered.

Before Raydon knew it, they were both inside their mate while she cried out in shock and pleasure. "Oh my goddess, shit, yes. Fuck me. Son of a bitch, what're you doing to me?"

Raydon laughed, amused at her inability to catch her breath but still able to cuss. "Hellmouth is a very apt name for you, love. You ready for us to move, or you need more time to adjust?" River asked.

She shook her head, her body following with an all over shiver. "I'm ready for more. Oh." her eyes widened as River pulled her into a sitting position, his brother's hand slid down her front until he found the little bundle of nerves. He thumbed her clit until she was squirming on his cock, making her moan and ride them both.

"Holy shit, yes, ride me. Fuck our cocks just like that, Sky." Their movements became jerky, nothing coordinated, or orchestrated as they all raced toward the edge. Finally, the bliss they sought crashed over them, snapping almost painfully through their shared link, rocking through Raydon, Sky, and River, sealing them together. Raydon sat up, his teeth sinking into his mark on the side of her neck. At the same time his brother bit the other side. Another shocking wave of ecstasy washed over them until they fell to their sides in a heap on the bed.

River pulled out of Sky first, then Raydon followed at a much slower pace, his dick felt perfect snuggled up in her tight pussy. Hell, he was sure he'd feel in heaven snuggled in any part of their mate.

Sky moaned while River rained kisses on her neck and shoulders. Raydon trailed kisses over her cheeks, lips, jaw, anywhere he could reach, he kissed. "That was better than I'd imagined," Raydon promised.

Her eyes fluttered open. "I agree."

"You're ours forever and ever." River's hands moved down her hips, then back up to her breasts.

"I'm glad, because you both are mine forever and beyond. I've never been so happy. I didn't think I could be, didn't think I was...worthy."

"Love, there's beauty in everything, even pain," Raydon said. When Sky tried to pull back, he held tighter. "When we suffer, but come out stronger, that's beauty. On the outside, you were always gorgeous, but after the fire you rose from the ashes a great beauty like you always were but didn't see it. If we could, River and I would take away the pain, but knowing everything you know now, would you want us to?"

She bit her lip, making him ache to slide into her again. Seconds turned to a minute before she finally answered. "I never thought of it like that. Not that I think I'm beautiful. Oh, I think beauty is in the eye of the beholder, and for that, I'm damn glad. Taryn and Joni, they're lookers with their curvy bodies and...eep, alright, I'll stop."

"When you love someone, it doesn't matter what the surface looks like. River and I are your mirrors. Let us give you a little more clarity. There's a light that shines within you, a light that even Stella hoped was going to lead her out of the darkness," River twisted her around until she faced him. "You're beautiful when you smile. There's no doubt we're not worthy, but we'll love you with everything we got and work everyday to make you smile, to hear you laugh. You see, that smile, its like the sun coming up for us. You make us whole. Having you in our lives makes us better men. We are so far from perfect, but we'll give you our best." River kissed her.

"Damn, you done went and broke my heart and put it back together again," Sky cried.

He grinned, loving her with every fiber of his being. Life might throw a lot of shit in their paths, but together, the three of them would jump any hurdles together. "Sky, in life, we're given only what they say we can handle. Well, fuck that shit. You have two mates who are here to help shoulder whatever comes your way. We'll all learn from experiences together. We'll make memories together, so in the years to come, we can celebrate and cherish them like a proper family. Our life is going to be a journey we walk together, hand in hand, not fighting step by step. I want to fill you up with so much love it makes all those bumps, curves, and hurdles worth the journey," Raydon whispered, moving her hair back while he kissed behind her ear, making goosebumps break over her flesh.

"I love you, the both of you." Sky wriggled until she was on her back, facing the ceiling.

River licked his lips. "It's my turn to be in that tight pussy, love."

Sky scrunched up her nose. "Shower first?"

Raydon shook his head. "Fey magic, love. Think it and it shall be done," he whispered.

The instant the words registered, her eyes widened. "I could've used magic to...to make it easier earlier?" She blushed after speaking.

He fell back, laughing long and loud, River doing the same.

"Hey, that's not funny. How would you like it if I shoved a baseball bat up your ass and...well, you'd need two holes for me to compare, but yeah, that," she huffed.

Raydon wiped his eyes, then pulled Sky back on top of him, keeping his dick from sliding back into her pussy. "Are you asking how we'd feel in your position if we just realized we could've eased the first time? Love, I'd have wanted it exactly how it was. It was perfect, to me. Did we hurt you?"

"No."

"Does your body ache to feel us possessing it again?" He could smell her sweet arousal perfuming the air, and she knew it.

She nodded but didn't answer.

With a firm swat to her butt cheek, he growled, "Answer me."

"Yes," she growled back.

"Good girl. Now kiss me. If you're too sore to make love again, then we'll shower and go to sleep. We have the rest of our lives to be together."

River waited until his turn, then he kissed her, echoing Raydon's words. They'd never make their mate uncomfortable in body, mind, or spirit.

"Your wants and needs are always the most important thing to us. We won't get satisfaction if we know our mate isn't," Raydon assured her.

Sky knew all she had to say was no and both men would stop. Oh, they'd still love her and make sure she was comfortable, but they wouldn't make love to her, and lord, she wanted to feel them inside her again. From her experience with Keith's pack, the animals there didn't give two shits about the females. It was all about them and their nuts.

"I want you in me." Dirty, sexy men. She definitely hit the lottery on her mating.

River growled. "Ah, hellmouth, we're the ones who are the winners with our sexy as fuck little mate. Let me have her, Rye, it's my turn to fuck that tight little pussy."

Her face had to be as red as a fire truck, darn her inside voice being so damn loud. She went into River's arms while Raydon got up, choking back a squeal as he began moving them to the edge of the bed. "Easy, love, we're switching it up a little," River said, grinning widely.

She straddled his thighs while he guided her back onto his cock, lifting her up and down.

"Damn, I think I love her ass as much as her pussy." Raydon grabbed both cheeks of her ass and squeezed. "One thing you need to understand, Sky, we will always want inside you, whether it's your pussy, your mouth, or your ass. However, your comfort will always be our priority."

"It is?" She gasped and looked over her shoulder to meet his gaze.

Raydon nodded, running a lubed finger up and down the crack of her ass, then there were no more words as he worked his magic preparing her for him.

He grinned, his eyes bright with arousal. "Oh yeah. Now, it's my turn to slide inside your ass. You ready for me?"

"Goddess, fuck me, now," she moaned.

Hours later, she lay between River and Raydon, listening to their breathing, their hearts beating in the same rhythm as her own. The completed bond sealing them as a triad mating settled her and the beasts within her.

"*Sky, you awake?*" Joni asked through their link.

She tried not to wake the guys, hoping her startled jerk hadn't woken them. "*Yeah, what's wrong?*" Thoughts swirled through her mind at why her friend was contacting her so late, then the memory of her at the movies with the strange shifter had her easing out of the bed, using the magic she'd been gifted from Lula.

"*I need to talk to you. Can you meet me?*"

She'd always been able to read Joni's tone, this time being no different. It was then she remembered they'd not gotten to speak at the movies thanks to the exorcist thing, damn chimera twin shit. *"Tonight?"*

"Yeah. Sorry, it has to be tonight. I won't be here tomorrow."

Fuck, that sounded all kinds of ominous. *"Where are you?"*

"At the elders' clearing. It's peaceful here."

Sky looked at her two sleeping mates, thought of waking them to go with her, then remembered she had a motherfucking wolfagon in her. *"I'm coming. Is anyone with you? Where's Atlas?"*

"He's gone back to his clan to be mated and create the next alpha cub. I can't do it anymore, Sky," she sobbed.

Feeling the absolute desolation through the space separating them, she raced through the forest toward Joni, putting as much speed through her wolven body that she could. Reaching out to Taryn, she pushed the entire conversation out to her. No way were they going to lose one of them. They didn't survive that bastard Keith only to end up...no, she wouldn't even think of the alternative.

She leapt over downed trees. The snow crunched beneath her paws, making parts of the trip slippery yet didn't slow her. When she reached the clearing a fire burned in the pit, highlighting Joni in human form. "Damn, girl, you're fast. Must be that dragon in you." Joni shivered, her arms wrapped around her body.

Sky shifted, moving to sit next to her friend. "What the hell you doing out here in a dress? Not that this isn't a gorgeous frock, but...it's a dress and it's winter." She plucked at the short hem of Joni's gown.

Joni shrugged. "I got dressed up for our date, but it was really a meeting. I...goddess, I'm pathetic. I can't pick a wolf, and I can't seem to pick a bear either. What's wrong with me, Sky?" she cried.

Her arms automatically wrapped around one of her best friends, feeling the tremors that wracked her frame. "He's clearly the loser 'cause you're Grade A, while he's a total reject."

Joni snorted. "Are we reduced to referring to ourselves as meat again?"

Noise from behind them had Sky pushing up and standing in front of Joni, her body poised to shift. Taryn walked out. "Oh, you gonna burn me with your laser eyes? At ease wolfagon," she teased.

"Did you call in reinforcements?" Joni asked.

Sky shrugged. "I figured we'd picked her up enough times. It was our turn to pick you up."

"Plus, if I'd have found out you beotchs were having a girls' night without me, I'd have kicked both your asses," Taryn mock growled, coming over to where they sat, bumping Joni's hip until she scooted over, giving her room.

"Gah, does this seem familiar?" Joni asked staring into the flames.

Taryn held her hands up to the warmth. "What, the three of us sitting outside in the cold, one of us hurting while the other two takes care of her? Then the answer is yes."

Joni bumped her shoulder. "No, the three of us together. Only we don't have to fear that one of our parents might find us and...well, you know." She wrapped her arms around her bare arms.

"Here." Taryn shrugged the coat she had on off and put it over Joni. "We could always shift and lie around in our wolven form."

"No, I like this. I feel normal. I have something to tell you, and I'm going to need you both to listen, don't interrupt, and don't try to change my mind. Okay?" Joni stared straight ahead.

"How can we agree without knowing what you're going to say?" Sky asked, turning to try to search Joni's features in the flickering firelight.

"Just say it, and we'll see how the chips fall, Joni. You're not going to get a promise from either of us, so deal," Taryn growled.

Sky loved her friends. Loved how Taryn was all alpha female who took no shit, and usually Joni was as well. So, she waited. Finally, her friend got up, Taryn's jacket falling to the ground.

"I'm leaving the pack. I...I don't fit with shifters, of any kind. Hell, I go into town and humans are nice to me. The guests at the lodge are nice to me. You two are the exception. I can't go the rest of my life searching for something that isn't going to happen. I'm not like you, Taryn, or you, Sky. The Fey didn't grace me with anything extra other than parents who hated me on sight. Hell, Keith didn't even glance in my direction, which I'm glad, but don't you think that's odd in and of itself? Don't you see, even the wolves of the Mystic Pack don't see me. Oh, they give me a passing 'Hi, how are you?', but that's it. Out with the humans, I might have a chance at finding love. Watching the both of you find that precious thing, that can't be bought and sold like so much garbage, I realized I needed it too. I thought I didn't, but I do. Watching Atlas walk out of my life made me realize I'll die if I stay here," she cried, tears falling from her glowing green eyes.

Sky got up, closing the gap between them, with Taryn next to her. "Joni, you know we can't let you leave. You're pack. You'll not survive out there all alone."

Their friend swiped at her tears angrily. "You don't understand. I'm fighting for my life here. If I stay, you think you're keeping me safe, but you're not. I'm not asking for more than I'm worth. I just don't want less. What I have now is less. I have nothing," she whispered.

"Where will you go?" she asked, knowing Joni probably already had it all worked out.

Her friend took a deep breath. "I'll let you know when I get there, okay?"

It was the only promise she was going to give them. "You have money?"

Joni's lips turned up into the first half smile. "My parents are computer geeks. You think they didn't teach me, inadvertently, some tricks?"

Shit, Sky so didn't want to know. Yes, she did. "Joni, please tell me you didn't do anything illegal or anything that's going to get you arrested?"

"Okay. Now, your two mates are waiting beyond the trees," she told Sky. "Taryn your dancing man is too. Go, be with them and be happy. I didn't want to disappear without letting you both know in person. A text or email is so passé." Joni flipped her midnight black hair behind her shoulder, it's length almost to her rear.

Jett stepped out first. "Why I gotta be the dancing man? You'd think I got nekkid and stripped for a living. Oh, I guess I've done the first two, just not for a living. Two outta three and all that. I know the girls are all for letting you go and make your way, but sorry, little girl, we can't let you run off on your own."

Joni shrugged. "You can protest all you want, but the reality is, you ain't my boss. TTFN, best friends."

Sky and Taryn were left holding air as Joni shifted, her sleek wolf disappearing faster than they could track.

Jett gasped. "What the fuck did they do to you all?"

River and Raydon prowled into the clearing, their worry wafting off of them in waves. Sky waited for them to come to her, knowing they'd woken while she'd been gone and feared she'd been hurt or worse. "I assume they had to hone all the skills at their disposal to survive." Raydon was the one to speak, but River's eyes said he agreed.

Sky and Taryn nodded.

"Joni always shifted fast, faster than we did, even as pups," Taryn whispered, looking toward the direction their friend took off. "Our link is closed, like she...severed it."

"I know, I felt it. She'll be okay, I can feel it." Sky held her hand out to Taryn, her lifelong best friend's pain had once been something she dreaded, because she too had to suffer the same, silently.

"We'll be here for her when she needs us." Taryn's voice shook. "Like you both were here for me."

"Let's go home, I've contacted Niall. As her alpha he should be able to track her." Jett wrapped his arms around his mate. Taryn leaned back, letting him take her weight as a mate should.

As Sky did the same with her own mates, she realized that was what Joni was wanting, needing. She wanted to be someone's treasure, not just another diamond in a line of diamonds.

"You're our greatest treasure. The rarest diamond doesn't compare to you," River promised.

They went back to their home, making love for hours, showing her that deep down it didn't matter what they had, just as long as they were together. Love is more precious than all the money and riches in the universes. Love can't be bought and sold, but thanks to her wicked mates, they'd shown her what it means to be truly loved. Long, hard, slow, deep and every other way there was to be loved.

His Sexy Wolf

Mystic Wolves 7

Joni shifted back to human just shy of the road, her senses on high alert. She'd bought the little Toyota Celica because it got great gas mileage; it would run forever, and it was the absolute last vehicle anyone would think she'd own. Plus, it was cute and sporty. She considered that a win.

Shoot, she was doing it. She was leaving the last pack. Well, it wasn't like she'd had a lot of packs to call her own, only two, but still...she was going lone wolf. The thought made her stomach flip and her wolf howl. "Shut it, you little bitch," she muttered and reached under the front fender for the extra key to the car. She'd been planning her escape from the pack for a long time. Although, to be fair, the Mystic Pack wasn't bad. To be honest, if things had been different, if she'd been different, she might have loved it. However, she wasn't different.

"There's no use crying over things we can't change. So buck up." The key slid into the driver's door, unlocking the little sporty vehicle. She settled into the leather seat, exhaling loudly at the cold that met her bare legs. Damn, she probably should've thought of different clothes when she'd shifted. Her pity party didn't call for warm clothes, though, she reminded herself. The memory of why she'd been dressed in one of her favorite little dresses made her heart ache. Damn Atlas and his sweet sexy bear self. She'd been so sure he was it for her. Her wolf had even whined and rolled over for him. Oh, she hadn't allowed him to fuck or make love to her. No, Joni was saving that for her mate. Of course, Taryn and Sky didn't know that. Or maybe they did.

"Enough, Joni. Get the hell outta town, girl." She put her seatbelt on, then twisted the key. The soft purr of the engine reassured her she hadn't bought a lemon. At least she'd done something right. If only Atlas wasn't a bear, promised to marry another bear. Stupid bear politics. Just because his family was richer than sin, they expected him to mate

163

some perfect six-foot bear bitch and make perfect bear cubs. Goddess, she sounded like a twat, and she was not a twat.

She'd told him she wished him well, and she almost meant it. Even when regret had shown in his chocolate brown eyes, she'd wished him a happy mating and lots of adorable cubs. However, the thought of him making love to someone other than her made her wolf want to claw the unknown woman's eyes out. Stupid, because a bear and wolf fight would only have one outcome, unless it was one bear against a pack of wolves.

Joni flowed into the strangely busy traffic on the highway, heading South. Bears lived North, so she was heading South. Warm weather where lots of humans lived. This time next week she'd be sipping daiquiris on a beach with a tan. That's her plan, and she's sticking to it.

Dark Embrace

Want to read Jenna's Story?

http://bit.ly/2DZiLyWDarkEmbrace

Jenna rolled to the side, the taste of copper filling her mouth making it hard to swallow. She squinted, trying to figure out where she was without making too much noise. The room was huge. Like something out of a fairytale. The thought had the breath freezing in her throat. Her hand went to her cheek, feeling for the cut that had burned like acid soaking straight to her bones. When her fingers felt nothing other than smooth skin, she exhaled, hoping it had only been a nightmare. "Then where the fuckity fuck am I?" she whispered into the quiet of the room.

Shoving the blanket off her legs, Jenna scooted to the edge, her first thought was to blink her way back to her realm now that her mind was clearing. With every inhale of breath, she knew her guys were near, but she couldn't get a clear read on where exactly. Damien and Lucas Cordell, the princes of, well, she wasn't exactly sure what as their father was the Vampire King who was mated to a wolf shifter. Being the eldest of their children, and twins, she guessed they were next in line to take over if he should ever step down. The last time she'd seen the powerful king, he was no closer to releasing his title than she was. Being the Fey Queen for thousands of years was something she was proud of, yet it was also a burden. The memory of the time when the Goddess had revealed herself to Jenna came flooding back to her in a rush, making her feel lightheaded.

The garden of the Goddess was always a place Jennaveve felt she could go to when life, or more aptly, the fighting, became too much. Today, she was bone weary of all the warring between her kind and the others in the Fey Realm. Watching friends become enemies. Lovers become the complete opposite as they, along with families, destroyed each other, all over their thirst for power. The need for more. Always more, whether it was magic or land, it was always bloody and filled with the stench of death, and she was tired of watching, waiting for it to come to her door. "Dear Goddess, I'm ever so tired," she sighed.

"Ah, my sweet Jennaveve, you are far stronger than you give yourself credit for," a lilting voice whispered over the lilac fields.

Jenna jerked into an upright position, searching around her for the source of the voice. Oh, she knew who the speaker was, had heard the Goddess in her head hundreds of times in the three centuries she'd been alive, but not once had she actually thought to hear it out loud. Maybe she was hallucinating?

"You are quite lucid, child," the Goddess laughed. The sound like silver bells, only much more—magical.

She wasn't sure if she should stand, or kneel, or bow. Heck, she wasn't sure which direction to face or if she should face the ground and beg for forgiveness. Her entire body quivered out of fear. What had she done to bring notice from the Goddess?

"You should do none of the above, my sweet. Sit, let's take a moment and enjoy the quiet before the storm." The Goddess's soothing voice was like a caress.

Her mouth went dry as she stood. "I'm sorry for...interrupting your space," Jenna sputtered. Dear Goddess, she was speaking to the Goddess. Holy crap! A golden glow became almost solid, projecting the most beautiful form Jenna had ever seen, eclipsing everything else and stealing her breath as she stared.

The Goddess waved her hand. "No apologies. Sit with me."

Fear had her doing as she was told without question. The ethereal woman sat next to her, their legs almost touching as she took a blade of grass between her fingers. "What would you wish for if you had just one wish, Jennaveve?"

A lump formed in her throat as she thought of what to say.

"There is no right or wrong answer, only the truth," the Goddess instructed.

Knowing the being next to her would know if she didn't speak from the heart, Jenna licked her lips. Her mind spun. The first thing most would ask for would probably be power, but Jenna didn't crave the same as the rest of her kind. She'd always been different, which made her more of an outsider in many, if not most, circles, even in her home with her family. What she truly wanted, if she could have one wish, was something her Fey family would scoff at, but in her soul, was what she yearned for. Without hesitating, she took a deep breath, taking in the sweet scent of lilacs, and released it. "I want to be able to rest without fear and have my people do the same each night."

A golden hand brushed lightly over the top of her head, making the tension that had invaded her as she'd spoken ease. Instant lightness flowed through Jenna. "All my children should feel this way," the Goddess agreed. "This is why you were born to be queen. You, my sweet Jennaveve, are my greatest creation. You are destined to be the Queen of the Fey Realm. From this moment on, you will be the one to bring peace to all of Fey, and with my powers inside you, you'll be the strongest, most powerful being in all the realms."

"I don't...what do you mean?" Jenna whispered, her throat barely allowed the words to come out as knowledge began to flood her. A strange power pulsed within her veins.

"All of the beings here in Fey are my children, but you my child, you were created with more. You are a part of me, created by me, from me, for this purpose." Her lilting words were filled with power. The Goddess ran her palms around Jenna, speaking words that Jenna couldn't interpret, but as the last words rang out, a surge had Jenna crying out, forks of white hot power sent her falling onto her back.

"What's happening to me? We are all your children," she gasped out. More knowledge and power filled every fiber of her being, shredding her from the inside out. Jenna feared she was going to explode as the pain increased.

"It's okay, Jennaveve. I'm sorry for the suffering you are feeling, but it's almost done. The power has always been inside you. I just needed to unlock it." The Goddess shook her head; a tear rolled down her cheek completely unnoticed by her.

The urge to reach up and wipe the moisture away had Jenna trying to lift her arm, but the movement was too much effort.

"See, that is why you are the Queen. Yes, all here are my children. However, many years ago, too many for me to recall, I had a vision. In it, I saw the need for one such as you. In the way of my kind, I created what I knew would be the savior of this realm and beyond, then waited for the right time. You needed time to...well, for lack of better terms, experience enough of life to mold you into what you needed to become, before bestowing the mantel of what you were destined to be. That time is now, Jennaveve," the Goddess said, her words echoed around them with authority.

Finally, as the pain was subsiding, and she no longer felt as if her body was being shredded, she was able to take a deep breath without feeling like thousands of knives were digging into her. Moving her head didn't take as much effort, so she rolled her neck to the left and looked at the Goddess who was sitting calmly staring off into the distance. "What do you want me to do?" As the last word left her mouth, the Goddess touched her forehead, more knowledge filled her head like a tsunami. Then, just when she was sure her brain was going to explode, the pressure was gone. The bright rays of the dual suns were replaced by the two moons.

"It is time for you to rest now, for tomorrow you will show all what it means to have you as their queen."

Jenna could only blink, or at least she thought she did. However, the last thing she remembered was loving arms lifting her from the ground, wrapping around her and rocking her back and forth, gently, like a mother would a child. Words that sounded like a song floated through the air singing her to sleep. For the first time in hundreds of years, Jenna rested without fear.

~Present Day~

As her feet touched the ground, her legs wobbled then gave out. The feel of the cold tile slapping against her palms had her crying out even as her knees slammed into the unforgiving surface. "Shit," she moaned.

Why nobody had come at her cry was a little alarming, but it gave her a moment to get her bearings and stand up or attempt to stand. Hell, she'd take leaning on the bed while standing on her two feet at the moment as a step in the right direction. "You can do this, Jennaveve," she cheered herself on, but in all reality, it took more effort than she'd thought. "What the hell happened to me?" A fine sheen of sweat covered every inch of her body like she'd been working out for hours.

She remembered allowing herself to be kidnapped by a scumsucking vampire freak who'd mated with a panther shifter. The jackhole had wanted to kill his wife while his daughter watched. In his mind, which she still wanted to gag when she thought about the things she'd seen in his memories, the bastard wanted to teach his daughter a lesson or something. She rubbed at her temples as she thought back to the night in question.

Yes, she'd only been in his clutches for a couple hours. Her Iron Wolves were coming. She remembered sensing them, along with Damien and Lucas. Everything was going according to plan, until a stranger came out of the darkness.

Fear had her looking around the quiet room, opening her senses in search of the being who'd come out of nowhere that night. His essence reminded her of the Cordell's only darker. Sinister. Goddess, she'd never felt such a being before and didn't want to ever again. A shiver stole up her spine. "Please tell me I'm not his prisoner?"

No, she couldn't allow herself to think that way, or she'd lose whatever sanity she had left. She needed to get to the Fey Realm and recharge. Once she was back to herself, she'd return and speak, or mate, whatever the wolpires did. Jenna nodded, then opened her heart reaching for her home. When nothing happened, and she was still leaning against the large four-poster bed, real anxiety nearly felled her. "I'm just overly tired. Can someone come and help a girl out." Like before, she reached out for one of her friends, only a vast emptiness met her quest.

Never in all her years had she not been able to communicate with whom she wanted, when she wanted. Never had she been unable to move between realms. Until now.

The door opened to the right, it's slight creak like a shotgun in the quiet room. Jenna raised her right hand, preparing to defend herself. With what, she had no clue as she could barely stand on her own two feet, but she'd be damned if she'd go down without a fight. Of course, she'd probably go down in a stiff wind, but the young female who entered paused, her startled gaze appeared friendly.

"Good afternoon, miss. I came to check on you. We weren't sure you'd be awake just yet. Let me go get..."

"Who are you, and where am I?" Jenna demanded hiding the tremble that shook her by forcing rigidity into her body.

Eyes as wide as a baby doe, the girl kept one hand on the door. "I'll just go let the others know you're awake. Is there anything I can bring for you?"

Jenna wanted to run across the room and make the girl stay, but her body was shaking from standing already. "Please, tell me where I am."

"You're in the guest wing, of course. I'll just go tell them you're awake." The maid began walking out the door.

"Wait. Who are you going to tell?"

"Damien and Lucas of course." The girl bowed and backed out as if she thought Jenna was a crazy person.

Hearing the names of those who were destined to be her mates, had her relaxing. If she was in their home, then she was safe. They'd help her figure out why she couldn't access the Fey Realm or reach out to anyone. The way she was feeling, it was as if she was—human.

The air stirred near the large fireplace. What made her look she wasn't sure, only that she knew something seemed familiar. She expected to see Damien or Lucas, heck her heart actually sped up at the thought of seeing them. However, her body froze as the man from the darkness appeared. "What are you doing here?"

She whipped her head toward the door the young girl had gone out. Although Jenna's senses weren't on track, she was sure she'd been a human, especially since it was daylight. The being in front of her came out of the shadows, allowing her to get her first real glimpse of him without the cover of night or a trick of him keeping his identity hidden. Oh, he was gorgeous, there was no doubt of that. But what was most startling was his resemblance to Damien and Lucas.

"Hello again, Fey. You're looking slightly ill. Are my...family not treating you well?" His eyes flashed from obsidian to red. Where her men had gorgeous eyes that she wanted to get lost in, this mans were cold and lifeless.

His words finally registered. "Your family?"

He raked his claws together, making them clack in a way Jenna was sure he did to scare his victims. *Newsflash asshole, I've faced bigger, badder, uglier, and hopefully deadlier foes*, she thought.

"I'd love for us to stay here and chat, but I fear the big guy is waking, and well, I'm not in the mood for a reunion just yet. By the way." He looked toward the doorway. "Sorry, my pet. I don't usually use females as pawns, but in this instance, it's a must." He flew across the room, eliminating the space separating them.

Jenna fell back against the bed, nearly falling to the floor on her ass. His quick reflexes kept her upright. "What the hell are you talking about?" She pressed her hand to his chest, trying to put space between them.

He shook his head. "You'll find out in due time, my pet. Now, we must go before father-what-a-waste awakens."

She knew the telltale signs of magic and could feel it as the man in front of her began to manipulate the fabrics of time and space. "Who are you?"

He flashed her a smile, white teeth with two canines much longer than the others prevalent. "My name is Khan, son of Zahidda. Bastard son of Damikan at your service."

The door flew open, giving her hope she'd be saved. The sight of Damien and Lucas had her shoving harder against the rock hard chest. "Let me go, asshole. I'm not your pawn." It was like trying to move a mountain if you were a mere human. Goddess, she hated being so weak.

"Jenna, flash away," Damien growled.

"Ah, but your female can't. It seems I'm her cure, little brothers," Khan taunted.

Lucas stepped forward. "Who are you, and what do you want?"

Khan tilted his head to the side. "You have nothing I want. Tell your *father* I'll be in touch. Oh, here," he tossed a necklace onto the bed. "He'll know who I am with that. If not, then you're little plaything will become mine, until I tire of her."

Blackness swirled around Jenna as she heard both Lucas and Damien roar her name. A sick feeling hit her square in the gut, one she knew all too well. Goddess, the memory of the first time she'd come into contact with Damien and Lucas brought a shiver to her. Lucas had been injured and she'd been called to heal him. As soon as she touched him an electric shock had gone through the two of them until it had found Damien, connecting them for all time. The knowledge that they were hers, and she theirs was as clear as glass, but she'd held them off thinking she needed to fix what she'd deemed broken. Now, faced with the possibility of never seeing them again, Jenna cursed herself for being foolish.

Khan was playing a game with the Cordells. One only he knew the rules to, and he had zero compassion for anyone getting in his way unless he could use them for his own gain. Jenna just happened to be exactly what he needed in order to hit back at the man he felt deserved it. Shit, she so could use her Fey powers, or even her bestie Kellen right about now. Or even better, if she'd not been so stubborn and mated with Lucas and Damien, instead of waiting, then none of this would have happened. "Well, what ifs do nothing but make big girls cry over spilled milk," she muttered to herself.

"What?" Khan asked as he opened the portal allowing light to filter in.

She blinked a few times. "Huh?"

"You mumbled something about girls crying and spilled milk." He carried her over to a couch and set her down. His gentle touch and actions at war with his words to Damien and Lucas.

The light airy room reminded Jenna of a lake cabin, one that families would go to on vacation. "Oh, um, nothing. I talk to myself sometimes."

Khan shrugged his shoulders. "Make yourself comfy, you'll be here for a spell or two." He winked.

A growl rumbled in her throat. "Hahaha, very funny."

He was next to her in a blink. "No, I'm not funny at all. What I am is deadly. You'll do best to remember that." He raised his nails, the longer lengths looking ominous now, reminding her of the night he'd cut her cheek.

"You did something to me when you sliced my cheek open." If he was going to kill her, she'd at least know the hows and whys.

"I didn't realize I'd poison you the same as those ghouls. I spelled these." He clacked his nails together before continuing, "to kill with maximum efficiency. I thought I'd scented something different on you and was just going to take a taste. When I smelled my...the Cordell's blood in you, I realized the chance to finally exact justice on their father was now."

Her world righted itself as she realized why he looked and smelled like her men. "You're their brother?"

"Ding ding ding. Give the girl a prize." Khan walked away, his stride not quite as smooth.

"But, how? I mean, are you?" She was at a loss for words. She'd met Damien and Lucas's parents, Damikan and Luna, and couldn't imagine either of them giving up one of their beloved children. He'd called himself the bastard son, yet it didn't equate with the man who was known as the Vampire King, the one she'd met.

Khan turned around, his eyes glowing red. "Damikan seduced my mother then left her for his queen, the shifter bitch. My mother was ruined in the eyes of her clan, tossed out like trash since the Vampire King wouldn't acknowledge her or me, her bastard son. We had to fend for ourselves, fight for everything we could get, including the ability to sleep without fear we'd be staked at sunrise. All the while, his greatness lived in his grand home with his Hearts Love and created a new family, while me, his eldest son was a beggar in the streets. The things my mother had to do, in order to keep us safe until I was old enough to help, would turn your hair grey. Would you like me to tell you some of them, Fey?"

Jenna swallowed, knowing what he was implying. The thought of anyone, man, woman, or child being forced to do anything made her want to rip the nuts off of the ones who did the making. "No, I don't need the details. However, I don't believe for a second that Damikan knew. He's an honorable man."

No sooner had the words left her mouth before she found herself against the stone floor, an angry Khan looming above her. "You don't know anything. What have you ever had to suffer?"

She wanted to reach out with her powers and soothe his pain away, but had nothing except her arms, yet she didn't want to touch him. "I'm sorry, Khan."

He flashed across the room. "They'll come for you, and when they do, I'll kill them and then, Damikan will know what suffering is."

Jenna gasped, a spark of her powers flared to life at the thought of Damien and Lucas being hurt. "Over my dead body."

Khan raked his gaze over her prone form. "That can be arranged as well."

In a blink, he was gone, leaving her on the cold floor with nothing but a small bit of her former powers. "Goddess, wherever you are, help me please." The last thing she wanted was for her guys to try and save her, only to be hurt, or worse, killed in the process. Khan had powers that rivaled that of Damikan, only darker. No, she'd find her Fey spark and save herself, then somehow, she'd figure out what the fuckity fuck happened all those years ago. How the heck could Damikan have fathered a child, a son, and left him with his mother without giving both of them his protection? By her calculations, he was thousands of years old at the least since Damien and Lucas were over three millennia. Luna was going to rip his dick off. Jenna smiled in spite of her situation. It was either that or curl up in a ball and cry. It had been way too many years since she'd indulged in a pity party for one and didn't think this situation merited another one, yet.

Damien looked at the empty space where Jennaveve had been only moments before then at the shocked face of his twin, knowing his own reflected the same expression. "That couldn't be who it appeared to be." He paced away, his wolf scratched beneath the surface of his skin with the need to find their mate.

The bedroom looked as if an F5 tornado had been through it in the short amount of time since they'd entered and watched the bastard disappear with their woman. He knelt next to the bed, scenting Jenna's blood. A small smear of her precious life force coated the tile flooring. He ran his finger over the red stain, bringing it to his nose, inhaling, focusing on what had caused the injury. Instant jarring took him into the exact moment their Hearts Love had fallen onto her knees, her cry of pain was like a blade slicing through his own heart. "Why did one of us not stay with her?" Anguish and regret filled him.

Lucas's roar had the windows rattling, his wolf every bit as angry as Damien's. "I don't understand this, but we were only away from her for short periods of time. Whoever...that being was, he knew when to strike. It was as if he had a connection to her. He looked like us."

Distaste soared through Damien. He glared at Lucas, wanting him to take the words back. Their Jennaveve didn't belong to anyone but them. "We must summon father. This happened in his household. Surely he has a way to track whoever came and went."

His brother's eyes flashed blue. "Whoever he is, he's a dead man."

Damien nodded. "In that, we agree."

The door flung open, wind pushing him and Lucas backward as Damikan entered, their mother Luna rushing in behind him. "What the hell is going on? First, I feel a breach in my wards, and then I'm summoned," he paused, pointing at his chest. "Me, summoned to a guest suite as if I'm not the King. You have thirty seconds to explain before I teach you and your brother why I am the ruler." The air crackled with power.

It took all his control not to cower in the face of his father's fury as the King of Vampires blasted his dominance at them, the very air became heavy, threatening to push him to his knees. He and Lucas both stayed on their feet, fighting the power, holding their bodies straight by sheer will. Blood seeped from his nose, but he wasn't willing to show any weakness, not now, not when Jenna's life was on the line.

"Enough," Luna yelled, stepping between them, holding her arms out. Their mother's head whipped back and forth, tears falling down her cheeks, blood ran from her nose as well.

"Someone took *our* Jennaveve from your home. He was right here, and he looked just like you." Lucas stabbed an accusing finger toward Damikan.

Damikan's deep rumble made the one Lucas had emitted earlier seem tame as he took a step forward. "What are you saying?"

Damien glanced between his mother and father. No matter how pissed he was, the thought of hurting his mom was something he didn't want to do, but Jenna's life was on the line. "Look into my memories," he said instead of speaking out loud, thinking their father would rather see it first then explain to their mother.

"Oh no you don't," Luna spat, blood on her face from where Damikan's dominance had pulsed through the room.

Their father broke his gaze from them, sucking in a breath. "Luna, what...come here." His gentle tone at odds with the anger still simmering in the air.

Luna shook her head but moved next to him. "I want to know what's going on, and I won't be brushed aside. Speak, Damien."

With a nod, Damikan wrapped his arms around their mother. "Whatever you have to say, you can say in front of your mother. We have no secrets." As he spoke, his right hand went up and down her body, cleaning the evidence of blood from her.

Luna relaxed into his embrace, the strain melting away.

Lucas came to stand next to him, folding his arms across his chest. "This is the most fucked up thing we've ever encountered, and let me tell you, between the two of us, we've seen and done a lot. I know you've been together since you were both basically kids, and in our world, it's unheard of for two to find their Hearts Love so young the way you did, father. What were you, a couple hundred years old when you and mom bonded?"

Damikan nodded, his chin resting next to their mother's ear. Damien wondered how they were going to react to the next words that came out of Lucas's mouth. He looked over at his brother, waiting for him to finish. "Almost into my third century. Your mother was much younger, though. However, what does this have to do with what's going on here?"

Lucas shrugged. "I started, you get to finish, old chap."

"Fuck," he swore.

"Damien, really, was that necessary?" Luna asked.

Damikan growled.

Every moment they stood there and put the conversation off, the longer Jenna was in the other man's hands. "Use your senses, dad, tell me, us, what do you smell? Who did you sense when you entered? You felt the breach to your wards. Track the intruder and tell us who it was, or who you think it was. Then, I'll tell you who was here," Damien said a little less forcefully.

"Enough of these riddles, Damien. Your Hearts Love has been taken and you want to play games? If it were my Luna, I'd rip the very fabric of this world apart to reach her." His father's eyes flashed to obsidian.

Damian nodded. "It seems there was a woman before our mother who you must've felt something for since you gave her a son."

His words fell like stones dropping down the side of a mountain. Again, the pressure built in the room. His mother's gasp and shocked disbelief was clear on her beautiful olive complexion.

"What the hell are you talking about? I have no other sons." Damikan turned Luna to face him.

"He is not mother's child, but yours. Look into my memories. Both of you." Damien wasn't willing to force himself into his parents' minds, but he opened his memories for them, allowing them to see and hear what the stranger had looked like and said.

"How?" Luna asked, her hand covered her mouth, while the other went over her heart.

Damikan released her, moving around the room in a slow methodical way. His head tilting this way and that. When he reached the far corner near the fireplace, he stopped, inhaled deeply then disappeared.

"Shit, where did he go?" Damien tried to trace and follow, calling out for his father's elite soldiers as he did, only to come up against a solid shield, keeping him locked inside the castle. "No," he roared. They'd been able to trace since they were children, tracking their father should've been easy. However, he'd locked them inside the castle while he'd gone off, leaving them with a sense of betrayal.

At the same time his twin disappeared, then reappeared next to him, his fist bloody. "I tried to break out through the back gates, but he has us warded in. Why would he do that?" Lucas shook out his hands.

Pain and betrayal slashed at Damien, echoing through the twin bond he shared with Lucas. Looking over to where their mother stood, she seemed smaller, more fragile than ever before. He took a step toward her. "Mother...I," he stopped.

Luna held her head up. "Do not apologize for something you have no control over. We will get Jennaveve back, and I'll handle your father." Her eyes flashed blue, fur rippled over her and then, their human mother was replaced by that of her wolf. Anytime she needed time or space, she'd always told them she needed her fur. Now, was clearly one of those times.

"Fuuuck," Damien roared, his wolf and vampire halves battled within him. He wanted to shift to his wolven form and rip through the walls of the castle until he found Jenna but knew she wasn't anywhere near. The link that bound them was tenuous at best, and it seemed to be fading.

"What about the Iron Wolf? They have a...special connection," Lucas spat.

Walking over to the shredded bedding, he picked up what was left of the pillow case, pulling it to his nose. "I think I just threw up in my mouth, when you said that, but it has merit. Can you link with the asshole?"

Lucas opened his mind and concentrated on Jenna's best friend, Kellen Styles of the Iron Wolves. He knew the shifter had just become a father to quadruplets and truly, almost, in a slight way, hated to bug the bastard. However, he also knew if Jenna couldn't reach them, she would try to get into contact with the one she called her bestie. Yeah, like Damien, just thinking that way had him gagging. One day, it would be them she'd look at as her besties instead of Kellen.

Fuck, he was becoming a giant pussy thinking he wanted his Hearts Love to be their best friend. Shit, next he'd be scheduling them regular mani and pedi sessions together. Might as well wrap it up with facials with cucumbers over their eyes, too.

When the link didn't immediately connect him with Kellen, his fists clenched at his sides. He felt a pain behind his eyes as he strained harder. "Motherfucker, why would our father do this to us? It's like he's crippled us here while our woman could be..." He swallowed unable to continue speaking.

Damien waved his hand around the room, putting everything back to the way it had been when they walked in. They could erase the damage around them, but not the memory of watching her frightened face or the words that came out of the man's mouth. "He called us his little brothers. That would mean our father had him with another woman. Clearly, he's walking around during the day, so he's not a full vamp. Is he like us?"

Lucas thought back to the very beginning, rewinding it in his mind then allowing the scene to unfold in slow motion. The man looked almost identical to their father, down to his towering height and the obsidian eyes. Damien and he had blue eyes thanks to their mother but not him. Their father only had blue eyes when he became a wolf/hybrid, and that was if he wasn't angry. His memory latched onto the nails the other man had flashed. The sharp points looked as if he purposely made them sharper, longer. "He wants to appear sinister. Everything he did was to scare Jennaveve, yet his hold wasn't bruising. If he wanted to hurt our dad, killing her would hurt him, but it wouldn't truly devastate him. What is his end game?"

"I don't give a flying fuck what his end game is. I'm going to end *his* game," Damien promised.

He met Damien's stare, nodding. "If he's hurt one hair on her head, he's a dead man, brother or not."

"I'm going to bleed him for taking her and scaring her, no matter what blood runs through his veins, that's non-negotiable." Damien crossed his arms over his chest.

Lucas put his hands on his hips. "Stop looking at me like I'm going to argue, because newsflash, brother, I'm with you one hundred percent."

Damien put his hand out, waiting for Lucas to take it. "Jennaveve is ours to protect, ours to love, ours to get back, no matter the cost."

Lucas gripped his brother's palm, each one shifting until a single nail elongated, slicing into the other's palm, sealing the vow. "We will do whatever it takes to bring her back to us safely. Damned to all who stand in our way." Magic crackled between them as they both made the blood oath.

About Elle Boon

Elle Boon is a USA Today Bestselling Author who lives in Middle-Merica as she likes to say...with her husband, her youngest child Goob while her oldest daughter Jazz set out on her own. Oh, and a black lab named Kally Kay who is not only her writing partner but thinks she's human. She'd never planned to be a writer, but when life threw her a curve, she swerved with it, since she's athletically challenged. She's known for saying "Bless Your Heart" and dropping lots of F-bombs, but she loves where this new journey has taken her.

She writes what she loves to read, and that's romance, whether it's about Navy SEALs, or paranormal beings, as long as there is a happily ever after. Her biggest hope is that after readers have read one of her stories, they fall in love with her characters as much as she did. She loves creating new worlds, and has more stories just waiting to be written. Elle believes in happily ever afters, and can guarantee you will always get one with her stories.

Connect with Elle online, she loves to hear from you:

www.elleboon.com[1]

https://www.facebook.com/elle.boon

https://www.facebook.com/Elle-Boon-Author-1429718517289545/

https://twitter.com/ElleBoon1

https://www.facebook.com/groups/RacyReads/

https://www.facebook.com/groups/188924878146358/

https://www.facebook.com/groups/1405756769719931/

https://www.facebook.com/groups/wewroteyourbookboyfriends/

https://www.goodreads.com/author/show/8120085.Elle_Boon

https://www.bookbub.com/authors/elle-boon

https://www.instagram.com/elleboon/

http://www.elleboon.com/newsletter/

---

1. http://www.elleboon.com

Other Books by Elle Boon

Wild and Dirty

SEAL Team Phantom Series

Delta Salvation

Delta Recon

Delta Rogue

Delta Redemption

Mission Saving Shayna

Protecting Teagan

The Dark Legacy Series

Dark Embrace

51234393R00102

Made in the USA
Columbia, SC
16 February 2019